THE PASSION OF HADES

THE HADES TRIALS

ELIZA RAINE

ROSE WILSON

Editors: Christopher Mitchell, Kyra Wilson, Brittany Smith

Cover: Kim's Covers

For everyone who is convinced that there's a goddess of hell inside them...

ONE

PERSEPHONE

My head swam as I sat up, the sudden movement making me feel sick. But the nausea was replaced almost instantly by a surge of energy as I looked around myself, memories of what had just happened crashing over me in an endless wave. I was no longer in the ballroom, or the beautiful garden. I was in a plush bed-chamber, on sumptuous purple and teal cushions, sheer material draped decadently around the four poster frame that surrounded me.

I should be dead. Hades' true form should have killed me. But the pomegranate seed...

'The judges must like you,' said a deep, lyrical voice. I snapped my eyes to the source of the sound, and Hera smiled back at me from the foot of the bed.

'What-why am I here? I need to get back to help that man,' I stammered. Hera's eyes flashed with fire.

'That man is long past your help. As he should be.'

'He just wanted revenge,' I whispered. 'A life for a life... I took someone from him.' My skin crawled as the image of the carnage in the ballroom floated before me. I felt sick again.

'Persephone, as the goddess of revenge I have an understanding for what drove him, but my empathy does not extend to those who would cross the gods. No mortal should be that foolish.' Her face was set and fierce and I felt a ripple of something deep inside me respond to her power.

'Are the gods really that much more important than everyone else?' I asked, my voice small. I knew I was being rude, but I was unable to keep the question inside. 'Are you really all so arrogant?'

Hera stood, the heels of her shoes clicking loudly as she did so. A blast of power rolled through the room and I suddenly wanted to worship her.

'If you are to retake your place as Queen of the Underworld someday, you need a serious attitude adjustment,' she said. A lump formed in my throat as the fears that had built up over the course of the ball welled to the surface.

'When I was a Queen, was I like the rest of you?'

'Yes.'

'I would have pulled that man apart, limb from limb?' I whispered, my eyes filling with burning hot tears.

'Your wrath had a less gruesome air about it, I'll admit,' Hera said, tilting her head to one side, 'but you were as vengeful as any of us.'

No. No, I couldn't believe her. But why would she lie? *It doesn't matter what you were before. What matters is what you are now.* I clung to the thought, forcing myself to calm down, holding my tears back.

'Well, I'm unlikely to win, so you needn't worry,' I said eventually, struggling to sit in the mass of soft cushions. I needed to get out of there. I needed to see Skop; make sure he was safe. I needed to work out what the fuck had happened and get my shit together.

'Oh no, Persephone. You are just as likely to win as Minthe. The judges must like you indeed, to give you the chance to win your power back.'

'They put my power in the seeds deliberately?'

'They must have, yes. How did you know to eat one? You clearly didn't know before the last Trial or you would have done so sooner.' Her gleaming eyes bored into mine, and distrust caused my shields to slam into place. I didn't know this woman. And even if she was Queen of the gods, I didn't need to tell her anything. Could my new power keep her out of my head?

My feelings must have shown on my face, because Hera gave a tinkling laugh, then sat down on the end of the bed again.

'If you don't want to tell me, fine. And in case you're wondering, Hades has a spell on the underworld that means nobody can invade another's mind. It's really quite annoying.'

My eyebrows shot up.

'Why has he done that?'

'Hades is not the god most think he is,' she said softly, and I was sure I could hear compassion in her voice. 'He has more respect for living creatures than you would imagine.' Hecate had said something similar to me, about Hades not being what people thought he was. And more than that, I had seen a side to him completely at odds with... whatever he had become when he slaughtered that man. A shudder rocked me.

'He would have killed me,' I said quietly. 'If I hadn't eaten the seed.'

'Yes. Temper is an uncontrollable thing, for mortals and immortals alike. He would never have forgiven himself either, which would have been a complete pain for everyone. I'm glad you survived.'

I frowned. What was her angle? I didn't believe for a moment she cared about me, but I wondered if she did care about Hades.

'Why am I here? With you?'

'I thought it best to remove you from harm's way. Hades will take a long time to calm down. And my husband, Zeus, is good at taking advantage of chaotic situations. I wouldn't want you caught in his web.' This time there was a dangerous glint in her eyes, and her voice held an edge to match. I imagined Zeus' glee at seeing Hades lose it so spectacularly, and anger pulled at my gut.

'How long do I need to stay here?' I asked her.

'Why, are you not comfortable?'

'I... I just... I wanted to see Skop.' There was a flash of

white light, then the kobaloi, butt-naked and sporting a look of complete confusion, appeared on the bed. He whirled, his bearded face sagging in relief when he saw me.

'Oh, thank fuck for that,' he said, then shimmered into his dog form. '*I thought you were dead.*'

'I'm touched you care,' I told him.

'*Are you shitting me? You saved my life.*'

'And you mine. I wouldn't have known what to do with that phoenix otherwise.'

'*Nor did I, Hecate told me to tell you. She couldn't reach you herself.*' I remembered seeing her during the chaos, her eyes milky, and blue power glowing around her. Gratitude heaved through me. She had been there, with me when I thought I was about to die. Begging Hades to stop.

Skop flopped down onto the bed with a massive sigh. '*I could sleep for a week after that,*' he said, his eyes closing.

'What a strange thing to grow attached to,' said Hera, one eyebrow raised as she looked at the little dog.

'He and Hecate are my only friends here,' I said, following his lead and leaning back on the cushions. If I was stuck here, I may as well get comfortable. I wanted Hera to leave, so I could work out this new energy flowing through my body. I didn't feel any different, but I knew it was there.

'Hades is your friend.'

I snorted involuntarily.

'Yeah, If you're into friends who can kill you, or like to wind you up to the point of exploding and then...' I trailed off, realizing my anger had made me say too much. A knowing smile crossed the goddess's dark, sumptuous lips.

'Well, now that you have a modicum of power, you might be able to survive long enough to make friends with him properly,' she said, far more gently. 'This place was very different when he was happy. I should like to see that again.'

Frustration simmered inside me, making my skin feel hot when it wasn't.

'Why won't anyone tell me why I left? Or what I did to that poor man's wife?'

Hera let out a long breath.

'He was telling the truth about you drinking from the river Lethe, you know. It is one of five rivers of the Underworld, and it will obliterate the memories of any who taste its waters. Only the King of the Underworld can reverse a power like that.' My hopes sank even farther into the pit of my stomach. Hades wouldn't tell me what had happened. He'd made that abundantly clear.

'Fine. Athena was right anyway, I should just move on. Worry about the future instead of the past,' I said, not able to give the words the sincerity I had hoped.

'He might tell you, you know. Should I send him to you?'

My jaw dropped slightly as dread trickled down my spine, flames already licking at the edges of my vision at the thought of how I had last seen the King of Hell.

'No! No, I... I think I should rest,' I said, too loudly.

'You can't avoid him forever. You're competing to marry him,' she said, then disappeared with a flash of white light.

I swore as I blinked the bright spots away. I was competing to marry a freaking maniac.

TWO

PERSEPHONE

As soon as I was done swearing about self-entitled douchebag gods, I sat upright again, and closed my eyes. If I had gained power, I needed to know what I could do with it. I concentrated hard, trying to feel something inside me that wasn't there before, that surge of life and vibrancy that I'd felt after eating the seed.

But I could feel nothing.

I knew it was there, the hairs on my skin rose when I thought about it, and Hera had confirmed it, but I couldn't feel that same surge of energy within me, or grasp anything tangible. Maybe I needed to try to do some magic? Feeling pretty stupid, I held out my hand.

'Light?' I awkwardly asked my own hand. Nothing happened. Why did I think I could create light? Hecate had said I had been able to 'grow plants, amongst other things.' I could feel, instinctively, that my power was connected to the earth. It was that same sureness I felt whenever I saw Hades' liquid-silver eyes, that same knowledge that everything I was experiencing wasn't a dream.

Hades' eyes... What in the name of the gods was I going to do? Panic fringed my thoughts as I pictured his face, remembered his passionate embrace, then saw that awful blue light roll off him and form corpses on the ground. I dropped my hand to my lap. I had been desperate to give every inch of my body to the man, less than an hour before he had turned into a freaking death monster, tore a man apart and nearly killed me. Worse, I was competing to *marry* him. This was no good. Like seriously, no good. I had to stay away from him, and I had to lose the Trials and get back home.

I couldn't ignore the surge of fear that accompanied that assertion, but it wasn't the fear I'd felt up to now. This was different. A brand new fear.

How the hell can you leave? This place is amazing! Maybe not the Underworld, but Zeus' mountain? Flying ships? Kick-ass outfits, magic everywhere, and a friend who could conjure wine for fuck's sake! Why would I ever go back to New York now I know Olympus exists?

'Because everyone here is fucking mental!' I said out loud, shaking my head and forcing the ludicrous thoughts out of my mind. 'Murderous fucking maniacs. And apparently, so was I!' I screwed my face up as I rubbed it hard with my hands. It was ridiculous to think I would even entertain the idea of staying somewhere so dangerous and unpleasant. *Somewhere I may once have existed as a monster.*

My brother Sam's face flashed into my mind, smiling

and soft. My parents, dad tending to the garden and mum sewing and rolling her eyes constantly, swiftly followed. I called up my more recent memories of Professor Hetz and my awesome garden design and the beautiful botanical gardens. I missed them. All of them.

'Manhattan roof gardens,' I said firmly. 'You're going to make this work, Persephone. You're going to become a world famous garden designer. Not Queen of the Underworld.'

But the last thing I saw, before falling asleep alongside Skop's snoring, furry little body were those desperate pools of silver.

I wasn't the least bit surprised when I found myself dreaming that I was in the Atlas garden. I walked slowly towards the fountain, inhaling deeply and filling myself with the scent of wildflowers. A warm breeze moved strands of my loose hair around my face, and it felt good.

'Thank you,' I said, as I reached the marble edge of the pool. Vivid green lily pads covered in shocking pink water lilies floated gently on the surface. 'You saved my life.'

'You're welcome,' the voice said. 'I am glad you are here. I must tell you something important.'

'Of course I'm here. You bring me here,' I answered, dipping my fingers into the water. It was cool and welcoming.

'I wish that were true, Persephone.'

'Oh. Well who does bring me here then?'

'I don't know.'

I tilted my head to one side, and felt the sun on my cheek.

'Who are you?'

'Your only friend. You must not eat all of the pomegranate seeds in one go. Do you understand me?'

'Yes,' I nodded.

'You deserve your powers back, dear girl, but you must not risk overwhelming yourself.'

'I don't feel overwhelmed. In fact, I don't know how to use my magic at all,' I said, reaching out and drawing a lily pad towards me while perching on the edge of the fountain.

'You will learn. Do not worry about that. But Persephone, you must trust nobody.'

'Except Hecate and Skop,' I said.

'No, nobody.'

'But Hecate and Skop saved me too. They care about me.'

'You are naive, little goddess. Hecate is an agent of Hades, and Skoptolis works for Dionysus. Only I work for you alone.'

'Why? Why are you helping me?'

'You were wronged, by my worst enemy, and you paid the highest price. And now only you have the power to make it right.'

A small shudder cut through the tranquility of the garden. His words carried weight that even this place couldn't lighten.

'I was wronged?'

'Yes. *The only person who can tell you about your past is Hades. And what he knows is incomplete.*'

'So... How do I find out the truth?'

'*When you are stronger, we will continue this conversation. Keep winning seeds, and gain more of your power back.*'

I nodded. That sounded like good advice.

The dream was vivid in my memory when I woke up in the opulent bedchamber, and I replayed the conversation repeatedly as I sat up in the mass of colored cushions, still wearing my ballgown from the night before. I rubbed my aching neck and tried to get the stranger's words straight. Could I really not trust Hecate and Skop? I struggled to believe they would bring any harm to me. I touched my parched lips as I looked down at the sleeping dog, sprawled across the end of the bed.

'*You were wronged, by my worst enemy, and you paid the highest price. And now only you have the power to make it right.*'

A little shudder rippled through me as I recalled the stranger's statement. If what he was saying was true, then was someone else involved in whatever I had done to get thrown out of Olympus? Did that mean it wasn't all my fault? A tiny bud of hope blossomed in my chest. But who? And why didn't Hades know about it? I blew out a sigh and stared at the glowing rock wall. At the thought of Hades, images rolled through my mind again, flipping between exquisite pleasure, and unbridled terror. Talk about an emotional roller-coaster.

'Well, this is nicer than your room,' said a voice, and my eyes snapped to the door.

'Hecate!' She smiled as she sauntered over, carrying two cups of coffee. 'Thank you, for telling Skop how to defeat the phoenix, and... for trying to stop Hades.'

'No worries,' she said with an overly casual grin. 'How you doing?'

'A bit confused,' I said.

'No doubt. But heh, at least your powers are working.'

'What?' I frowned at her. 'What do you mean? I was going to ask you how to get my magic to work; I can't do anything.'

'Persy, you got lifted five feet off the ground by a giant burning bird, fell and crashed into a table, and nearly got electrocuted to death. Don't you think you should be feeling a bit sore this morning?'

I stared at her.

'My neck aches,' I said eventually.

'That'll be these stupid fucking cushions,' she said, her lip curling as she picked one up and launched it across the room.

'So... My magic has healed me?'

'Yup.' She took a long swig from her coffee and I did the same, my mind spinning. I could heal?

'How?'

'It just happens while you rest. The stronger you are,

the quicker you'll heal, and you'll learn to heal big wounds on the spot eventually. You were always a good healer. Comes with the territory I guess.'

'What territory?'

'Goddess of Spring. New life. Growth and fertility and all that.'

My mouth fell open.

'Goddess of Spring?' I repeated, and heard a bark from Skop.

'Uhuh. No point keeping it from you any more, not if you can get your power back.' She was beaming at me, her eyes dancing with excitement. 'You can win this now, Persy. You really can.'

'*Woah, woah, woah. You're the goddess of fucking Spring? I thought you were just some pretty human?*' Skop's voice rang loud in my head.

'Erm, it's sort of a long story. I was married to Hades before. Then cast out of Olympus and removed from history. And I don't remember any of it.'

'*What the actual fuck?*'

'Yeah, I know,' I said to him with a look, then turned back to Hecate. 'What about what happened at the ball?'

'What about it?' she shrugged.

'Hades nearly killed me! I'm not marrying a god made of corpses!'

'Oh, he only lost his temper because that dude hurt you. When you're back up to full power his true form won't bother you at all.'

It felt like ice was sliding down my spine at her

words. How could that monster, surrounded by dead bodies, ever not bother me?

'I *want* to be bothered by corpses, Hecate' I told her. 'I don't want to be like him. I don't want to be with him.'

Hecate's smile slipped.

'He's just freaked you out a bit. You'll work it out, I'm sure.'

'Hecate, seriously, I'm not cut out for the Underworld. I want warm sunshine and a cool breeze, and trees as tall as buildings stretching into endless skies. I'm not meant to be here.' I could hear the pleading tone of my voice. 'Even if I was once happy here, I'm not that person any more. And Hades knows that.'

'You are not the woman I married. You are someone new.' That's what he had said to me, when I was practically delirious with lust.

Hecate stared at me for a full minute, then downed the rest of her coffee.

'When are you eating the other two seeds? We need to practice using your magic.'

I sighed.

'You can't just ignore me,' I told her. 'And I'm not eating them.'

'What?' she exploded, leaping to her feet. 'What do you mean you're not eating them?'

'Not yet anyway. I want to get my power back slowly.'

Hecate narrowed her eyes at me.

'Are you trying to lose on purpose?'

'No, but up until recently I was just a human, with no notion that magic even existed. You'll forgive me for being a bit cautious,' I snapped. She eyed me suspiciously.

'Fine, but I think you're making a mistake. The next round starts tonight, and you need all the help you can get.' My stomach twisted at her words.

'The next Trial is tonight?'

'No, not the actual Trial, it's just a little ceremony thing to start the second round and announce what's coming next. But Minthe will be there.' I groaned. Brilliant. Just what I needed. 'And... so will Hades.'

THREE

PERSEPHONE

Hecate zapped us back to my own room, and I gratefully stripped off my gown and stood under the hot water of the shower until my skin pruned. I tried again to access my supposed new powers, but other than a tingling awareness I couldn't get anything to happen.

'Was one of my powers making light?' I asked Hecate as I walked out of my washroom. She was sat at my dresser, one ankle crossed over her knee and her head back, singing something pretty.

'No,' she answered without looking at me.

'Oh.' I rubbed at my wet hair with a towel.

'*I can't make light either,*' said Skop in my head.

'You're not a god,' I told him.

'*I'm a god in bed,*' he answered, tail wagging. I rolled my eyes.

I got dressed in my fighting garb quickly, unable to keep still, my palms itching. I needed to do something physical; there was a pent up energy building inside me that was making me feel restless and uneasy.

'How long until this second round thing starts?' I asked.

'Ages, it's not until this evening'

'Good. I'm going to the conservatory,' I said.

'Oh. I thought you'd want to train,' Hecate said, tipping her head forward to look at me. I shook my head.

'Maybe later.'

'Fine, have fun. See if you can get those green fingers working some magic,' she said, and winked at me before shimmering out of my room. I looked down at my hands, wiggling my fingers. Could I get them to work actual magic?

It turned out that Skop had been telling the truth about paying attention to the routes through the underground maze I was living in. I would never have been able to find the conservatory without his directions. As we walked, I filled him in on what I knew about my past, which was a depressingly short conversation, and about eating the seed and my powers returning. I didn't tell him why I ate the seed, and he didn't ask.

I knew we were at the right door for the conservatory before I even laid my hand on the wood to push it open. Something was sparking inside me, and I could almost feel the plants on the other side of the wall, joyous energy rolling off them. My pulse quickened as I stepped into the glass room and inhaled the smell of soil. The restless energy thrumming through me transformed as I ran my fingers along the nearest yucca leaf, frustration morphing into excitement. *I could feel more than just these plants in this room.* Almost like little sparks of light in my mind's eye, I could sense seeds, unable to grow, trapped under invisible barriers that held them deep in the soil beds around me. I dropped to my knees and began to dig frantically in the nearest bed, hunting for what I knew was hidden there.

'Yes!' I pulled my hand up triumphantly, clutching a hard little seed.

'*What is it?*' asked Skop.

'A sunflower,' I said instantly, then looked sideways at him, drawing my brows together. 'How did I know that?' I asked slowly.

'*You're goddess of Spring. You probably should know a few things about flowers,*' he answered, then cocked his head at me. '*Can I do some digging too?*'

Together we dug through the huge space, turning almost all of the soil beds over in our hunt for seeds. There were so many, all hard and cold, as though they had been frozen in time. I found a tin tray stacked with the other tools and within an hour we had filled it with our unearthed treasure. They were mostly seeds for flowers; pansies and chrysanthemums and poppies, but a couple were more exciting. One I was pretty sure was an azalea but that would take years to grow. I certainly wouldn't see it reach maturity.

'Persephone.' Hearing my name made my body freeze as I knelt in the dirt, dread crawling up my throat as I recognized the voice. It wasn't the hissing tone, but I still had no doubt that it belonged to Hades.

'I thought you gave this room to me,' I said without turning. I knew my confidence would crumble as soon as I saw his dark smoke. 'Please go away.'

'Persephone, I'm here to apologize.'

'I don't care,' I lied. 'I have nothing to say to you, and there's nothing I want to hear from you.' All the hairs on my skin were standing on end, and the compulsion to turn around and look at him was almost too strong to resist.

'Please. Look at me.'

'No! Last time I saw you, you damn near frightened me to death.'

'I... I was angry. I lost control. You make me do that.'

'So it's my fucking fault?' I couldn't help the flash of rage, and I leapt to my feet as I whirled round. My anger dissipated instantly. There was no smoke. It was just him, his beautiful silver eyes glowing with sorrow. *Make it better. Make him happy.* The thoughts galloped through my brain and I snarled. Why was I so damned attracted to him? I tried to call up the image of the blue light turning into corpses around him, but he held out his hand to me and his lips parted, and heat rushed through my body. *Stop it! You don't fancy the lord of the dead, stop it!*

But my traitorous hand reached for his of its own volition, and he pulled me close to him.

'I thought you were going to die. I thought that man

would kill you. And Zeus wouldn't let me stop him.' His voice was so low I wouldn't have been able to hear him if his mouth wasn't inches above mine.

'Well, he didn't kill me. But you nearly did.'

He flinched and his grip on my hand tightened.

'A god's temper is his worst enemy. There is only wrath, no rational thought. I... I would never have forgiven myself if you had...' He trailed off, and his expression was so intense that I couldn't speak for the sadness that lodged in my throat. It was as though he was passing the emotion directly to me, through those incredible eyes. 'How did you know to eat the seeds?'

Alarm bells rang in my head at his question, snapping me out of the intense melancholy. *Trust nobody.*

'Never you mind. You need to tell me what happened before, Hades. I can't do this any more. I can't live a life I'm half blind to. It's not fair and it's driving me insane.' Hades lifted his other hand to my face, and very, very slowly drew his finger down my cheek. Pleasure coursed across my skin, and I tried to stifle my sharp breath.

'Would it make any difference if I told you that you chose to drink from the river Lethe yourself? You begged to forget what happened. And I promised you that you would never hurt like that again.'

Something fierce and painful surged inside me and I shook my head. *It was true.* I knew what he was saying was true.

'I don't care. It makes no difference now. I need to know.'

'I won't break my promise, Persephone. I can't.'

I expected to feel the familiar sense of frustration at being denied my own past once again, and opened my mouth to argue. But it didn't come. Standing so close to him was making my resolve soften, my distrust lessen, and my fear of him disappear completely. He loved me. I didn't know how or why, but nothing could be clearer as I stared into those swirling silver orbs.

'You said I wasn't the woman you married,' I whispered.

'Maybe not. But the bond between us is still there. And I can't fight it, no matter how hard I try. Especially not now you have your power back. You're like a damned beacon down here, impossible to ignore.' He ran a hand through his hair in frustration, looking for all the world like a normal, if impossibly sexy, guy.

'Bond?'

'Don't tell me you can't feel it,' he said, his eyes locking on mine. I wanted to tell him to stop being so arrogant, but I couldn't. He was right. There was definitely something between us, deep and real and damned inconvenient. *Corpses. King of the Underworld. Fire and ash and death. You do not fancy Hades!*

'Well, I don't think I've got it quite as bad as you,' I said as casually as I could. Fire flashed in his eyes, and I regretted my words immediately.

'Is that right?' he said, his tender, open expression vanishing and a predatory hunger replacing it. He seemed to grow in front of me, his shoulders filling out, his eyes flashing with desire. 'Let's put that to the test, shall we?'

Before I could begin to respond he had my face in his hands, and his lips met mine. Desire exploded through me, the hunger in his kiss even deeper than the last time. His other hand snaked down my back, his touch through the fabric of my shirt electrifying. I pressed myself into him, my back arching, my hands scrabbling at the buttons on his shirt.

But he stopped the kiss abruptly, stepping back and gripping both of my small hands in one of his. I started to protest but a wave of power rolled over me and all words abandoned me as I looked up into his face. Actual flames danced in his irises as his gaze raked over my body. The desire in his expression alone was enough to make my core heat, a low ache building inside me.

'I do believe, Beautiful, that we started on the wrong foot,' he said, his voice low and rich and sensuous. 'It appears that you have no idea what being fated to Hades, King of the Underworld, all powerful god, actually entails.' I stared up at him, panting slightly. *All powerful god.* My stupid, lust addled brain allowed my thoughts to slip between my lips before I could stop them.

'Does that mean magic sex?' I breathed. His mouth quirked into a smile.

'Magic sex,' he repeated, then a wave of pleasure began to trickle exquisitely across my body. It started at my neck, like the kiss of a feather, and as it moved lower across my chest I felt my nipples tighten and a gasp escaped my lips. Hades watched me, eyes dark and hooded, as the feeling rolled further south, the divine sensation dancing around my thighs but never quite reaching their apex. The ache was becoming unbearable, the need to be touched building into something that was making my legs shake.

Was this right? Was he making me feel this against my will? No. Hell, no. There was nothing I wanted more, and the longer I looked into his beautiful face, the more sure of that I became. *Fated*. The word he had used pulsed through my brain, interrupting the pleasure gripping my body.

'Stop,' I forced myself to say, and his expression flickered, before he let go of my hands, the waves of tingling pleasure, slowly lessening. He'd done as I asked. So he wasn't forcing his powers on me. 'Fated. You said I'm fated to you; what does that mean?'

He stared into my face, and I knew I must be flushed as I breathed hard. Desire was still gathering urgently between my legs, pounding and pulsing.

'The marriage of an Olympian god is not like a normal marriage. Hera, as goddess of marriage, has a special ceremony purely for us twelve.' I raised my eyebrows at him and he continued slowly. 'There's a test. And if both people pass, then they are granted the ceremony.'

'What test and what ceremony? Can you not answer anything properly?'

Hades clenched his jaw.

'I can't see the benefit of telling you.'

'How about because I fucking asked?' I said, the pent-up energy and tension inside me slipping quickly to anger. The corner of Hades' mouth quirked up into a smile again and I bared my teeth. 'Do I amuse you?'

'You just... Nobody other than you has ever spoken to me like that.'

'I don't care, just tell me about this ceremony.'

'No. Not unless you ask me nicely.'

My mouth fell open. Hades, the King of the Underworld, was teasing me. Well, two could play at that game.

I stepped close into him, standing on my tiptoes so that I could just reach his ear. He smelled like wood smoke.

'Pretty, pretty please?' I whispered, and flicked my tongue over his ear lobe. I felt him tense against me, then he gave a low chuckle and leaned his head towards mine.

'Oh, Beautiful, until you get your powers back, you'll lose this game every time,' he said, and suddenly that trickle of divine pleasure from earlier rolled over my entire body at once. Slick heat rushed my center, and my legs began to buckle. Hades wrapped one strong arm around my back, and as my hard nipples pressed against his chest I moaned again.

'Please,' I gasped.

'Please what?' His voice was hoarse and low.

'Please, touch me.' I was desperate for him, sure that only the slightest pressure would tip me over the edge.

'Not yet, Beautiful,' he breathed. 'I've waited twenty-six years for this, you can wait a little longer.' He brought his lips to mine, soft and full and intense. And then with a flash of light, he was gone.

I wobbled on unsteady feet as I blinked at the space Hades had just occupied. The waves of pleasure rolling though my body had vanished with him, but my burning need for him was still painfully present.

'For fuck's sake!' I exclaimed, digging my nails into my palms as I clenched my fists. 'Why did I let him do that?'

'Let him do what?' Skop asked eagerly, and my fired up body jumped in surprise at his voice. Embarrassment flared in me and I looked over at him, ten feet away in a soil bed, paws filthy.

'Oh gods, you must have seen everything?' I whispered, feeling my face heat.

'No, he put me inside a freaking smoke bubble. You look like you had fun though,' he said, and his tail wagged.

'Well, I didn't. And you're a weird little pervert,' I told him, relieved my encounter had been private.

'You've got no idea,' he answered, and launched back into digging up the soil.

'Skop, what happens when Olympian gods are married?'

'Mostly they cheat on each other.'

'Do they get divorced?'

'Nope. Never been an Olympian divorce.'

'So they just put up with the cheating?' A fierce stab of jealousy gripped me as I thought of Hades with another woman, and I scowled. Why the fuck would I care who he was with?

'Yeah.'

'Why? Why not leave?'

'*Dunno. Guess it's to do with them being immortal. It's not like they can just start hanging around with different friends, they all die after a bunch of years and then they're left with their ex again.*'

He had a point. That would be pretty awkward.

'I guess any affairs are temporary, for the same reason. The god would outlive any but their spouse,' I thought aloud. 'Wait, are all gods immortal?'

'*No. Only the Olympians. And the original Titans. Some of the strong ones, like Thanatos and Eris, can live until they are killed, but they're not true immortals.*' Well, that was interesting to know, I thought. The other gods could be killed. '*You know that's why the competition for Queen of the Underworld is so fierce?*' Skop said, his frenzied front paws stilling for a moment as he looked at me. '*Immortality is the most coveted thing in Olympus. And it's one of the perks of the job.*'

A strange feeling slid through my belly as I processed his words. Immortality? My brain seemed to fizz and cloud as I tried to imagine living forever, the idea too huge for me to deal with.

'People would marry someone they didn't love in order to live forever?'

Skop snorted and resumed his digging.

'*They'd do a hell of a lot worse than that.*'

I realized with a jolt that the strange feeling in my gut wasn't to do with the notion of *me* becoming immortal at all, it was to do with someone else marrying Hades for it.

Righteous indignation swelled in me, and anger made me stand up straight. Hades didn't deserve a woman like that. He deserved a woman who loved him, who would worship him as the king he was, who would make his every dream a reality....

Oh good gods, where was this coming from? He was made of death and smoke! *Come on Persy, death and smoke! He tore that man apart! Your brain is in your head, not between your legs!*

But he'd said fated... Could I be destined to be with him? Or did that just apply to the old Persephone, the one who had apparently killed another man's wife? A shudder rolled over me. This was all madness. I needed to stick to my plan. Lose the Trials, stay alive, and get back to New York.

FOUR

HADES

I paced up and down the breakfast room, flexing my fists and breathing hard.

Gods, I wanted her. And I knew how stupid it was to play with her, teasing and flirting and getting close. She would just be ripped away again.

But I couldn't stop myself. Even now, all the way in my rooms, I could feel her magic, a shining green light in the squalid sea of gloom I called home. I looked over at the platform where her tree had once stood, the branches blossoming over the table that was always set for two. For years it had been painful for me to come into this room. It had been our room. The place where we drank and ate and talked. And laughed. Her tree had softened the rocky room, bringing life and color and scent to the stillness. It had died the day she left, turning instantly to ash.

When Hecate had sent her here for lunch, and I'd seen her examining the rose and skull chairs, I'd wanted to seal the doors and never let her leave. *She was back.*

The one woman I had ever loved, and had thought I would never see again.

A moan of frustration left me, and I pushed my hand through my hair yet again, wishing my arousal would lessen so that I could concentrate. But her body, responding to me like she had...

She may not be the bold, confident Persephone I had married, but the kindness, the sense of right, the fire in her belly was all still there. As was Hera's bond. My destiny was as written in stone as hers was, but I had the advantage of knowledge. She had nothing but a load of gods telling her what to do, in a world she didn't recognize. I hated the idea of her anger and frustration, but how could I tell her what had happened? It had broken her once, and even if I hadn't made my promise to her, there was no way I would cause her pain like that again. And it wouldn't help her anyway.

There was a sudden urgent humming in the back of my mind, and I sighed.

'What is it?' I snapped. A voice in my head responded quickly.

'We have information on the man with the phoenix.'

Rage flamed inside me at the mere mention of the man who had tried to kill my soulmate, and I flashed myself out of the breakfast room. That was not a place for anger. *It was our place.*

I took my position on my throne, then summoned the speaker to me. He was the captain of my guard, a severe and enormous minotaur called Kerato. In fact, most of my staff were severe, and I often thanked the gods for Hecate and her much needed sense of humor.

'Tell me,' I said.

'He was named Calix, my Lord. He lost his wife in the incident and had begun a faction of sorts. He and an indeterminate number of others who lost loved ones call themselves the Spring Undead and it seems they spend their time looking for ways to avenge their fallen.'

Anger made my form swell automatically, fury edging the colossal power that burned permanently hot inside me.

'How the fuck do they even remember her? She was wiped from Olympian history!' Just saying those words was painful. *I wiped my own wife from history.* But I kept my face stoic in front of Kerato.

'We have been unable to find that out. It shouldn't be possible.'

'Unless they have access to the river Lethe.' Which would mean it was someone who was allowed to enter Virgo; one of the four forbidden realms and the most secretive place in all Olympus. That should narrow the pool of suspects down.

'We have only captured one more conspirator so far, and he died before we could get much out of him. We will keep searching for answers, my Lord.'

'Search faster, and next time you capture someone involved, I want to meet them personally.' Visions of tearing that man apart filled my head, and the heavy melancholy I normally felt when considering the dead was replaced with a gleeful wave of retribution. This was the part of myself I disliked most, but relied upon the heaviest.

This was all Zeus' fault. The thought of my brother only added more heat to my boiling blood.

He brought her back. *You got to kiss her again, feel her skin, hear her voice and see her glow.*

And I would have to lose her all over again. Just like the man I'd torn limb from limb, my heart would be torn apart, for a second time. Persephone had been right when she'd called him a colossal prick.

I waved my hand, dismissing Kerato. I needed to go and fuck something up, burn off this raging tension. I needed to get her out of my head. I was already regretting our encounter, the sight of her parted lips, closed eyes and heaving chest now impossible to shift.

I had to stop. It wasn't fair, on her or me. *Remember what happened. You can't keep a light that bright in the dark.*

FIVE

PERSEPHONE

By the time Hecate came and got me from the conservatory, Skop and I had found every buried seed. I'd spent a blissful hour sorting them into groups, then planning the flower beds. Lots of the seeds were useless, as they couldn't be grown indoors in the warm, or alongside other greedier plants, but a complex design was forming in my head that I was positive would be stunning if I could pull it off.

I had to shower again as I was covered in dirt, and then I got dressed in a gown that Hecate had chosen for me. It was a deep mossy green color, and had shoulder straps that slid down across the top of my arms and a boob-tube type bodice that skimmed the top of my breasts. I clutched at them, looking in the mirror.

'Are they actually bigger?' I asked Hecate as I peered down at my chest. She laughed.

'No. I told you when you first got here, you just needed better clothes.'

'*Or none at all,*' Skop chimed in. I ignored him. Working in the conservatory had definitely relieved some of the tension in my body from my encounter with Hades, but I still felt hugely restless. As soon as the word naked entered my head I was picturing Hades, bare and glistening and hard and...

I squirmed and shook my head.

'What do we have to do at this thing tonight?' I asked.

'Just have a few drinks, talk to a few folk, and find out what you have to do next in the Trials. It'll be a few hours, tops.' Hecate was wearing an electric blue dress that barely covered her ass, and had some sort of leather collar attached to the top. I wouldn't have been surprised if she produced a whip and handcuffs at any moment.

'Do you have a...' I tailed off, looking for the right word. 'Lover?' I finished a bit lamely.

'Hundreds,' she grinned at me.

'Anyone I know?'

'Nope. Now, are you ready?'

The Second Round Ceremony was being held in Hades' throne room, and when Hecate transported us there I felt a strange comfort in seeing the enormous colored flames licking up the open sides of the room. My eyes flicked to the thrones. There were only two empty chairs on the dais; the skull throne, and the rose throne. My gaze settled on the carved roses intertwined with the brutal thorns, and that spark of energy I thought might be my power rippled through my veins. I raised my eyebrows in surprise and stepped closer.

'Where you going?' hissed Hecate, and yanked my arm, spinning me around. I sucked in a breath. Fifty people or more were filling the rest of the throne room, all holding saucer shaped glasses and dressed in finery. Many I recognized from the ball, and Eros, that sexy-as-hell god of lust, stood out the most as he gave me a finger wave.

'Uh, hello,' I said, and a rumble of chatter started as they all turned back to whomever they were talking to before we had arrived. A few made their way towards us though, and Hedone and Morpheus were first to reach me.

'You did so well at the ball!' Hedone said, kissing me on the cheek. Pleasure rippled through me at her touch and I blinked, trying to dismiss the awkward feeling.

'Thanks,' I said, and took a glass from the little serving satyr's tray that had appeared beside me.

'It didn't go exactly to plan, but you handled it well,' said Morpheus, taking my other hand and kissing it.

Didn't go exactly to plan? It was a complete clusterfuck! A man was literally torn apart, because of me. I swallowed my real thoughts, plastering my practiced smile across my face and hoping it wasn't a grimace. This little get-together was going to be just the reminder I needed that these people were freaking nuts.

SIX

PERSEPHONE

'So, do you guys have any idea what's coming up next?' asked Hecate, and began to gulp from her glass of the divine fizzy liquid. I copied her.

'None. Although we have heard a little rumor about the last Trial of the Second Round,' said Hedone, eyes shining with excitement.

'Ooo, do tell?'

'I couldn't possibly,' Hedone said coyly. I clamped my teeth down on the inside of my cheeks to keep my smile in place. I seriously couldn't handle this shit. It was like secrets were currency in this place, nobody told anyone anything without making a great big deal of it first. A gong sounded and the chatter broke into a fevered buzz before dying out completely. I looked around the room for the smug pretty-boy commentator, and spotted him in front of the dais.

'Good evening Olympus!' he sang out. My eye twitched. 'Tonight we mark the start of Round Two of the

Hades Trials. Now, we'd better keep you all in the loop on what's been happening... Those seeds little Persephone asked for weren't just any ordinary seeds, folks! She's not as simple as she looks!'

'Hey!' I protested, but my words were instantly drowned out by his booming, amplified voice.

'Those seeds contained power! So our only human contestant is no longer at quite such a disadvantage.' He beamed at me as my mind raced at a hundred miles an hour. He knew about the seeds? He hadn't mentioned who I really was though, so whoever had told him was pretending it was new power, rather than my original powers returned. But why had they told everyone who was watching? The answer came to me straight away. If I suddenly did something magical in front of the world they would have a hard time explaining it. It would look like they had lied about me being human.

'And now, please welcome your gods!' With a blinding flash of light, the gods appeared behind him, their respective thrones shimmering into existence. My eyes were drawn immediately to Hades, his dark smoky form translucent and unnerving. I scanned the smoke for any glimmer of silver and found none. Shoving my disappointment deep into my gut, I looked along the row of thrones as I dropped to my knees and clapped with the rest of the crowd.

Aphrodite was impossible not to stare at, this time with snow-white skin, black lips and eyes, and baby blue hair cascading down her shoulders in a poker-straight sheet. She was wearing a sheer blue dress that split almost at her hip, and it was clear she had nothing on underneath. I felt heat in my cheeks, and forced myself to look on. Athena and Hera were dressed as they had been at the start of the First Round, traditional and serene looking, and Artemis and Apollo were both wearing gleaming gold armor in the style ancient Greeks wore in my books at home. Enthusiastic smiles shone out of their youthful faces, their amber eyes alive with excitement. Ares too was fully clad in war gear, as he had been before, and Hephaestus shuffled backwards in the same leather tabard.

But Poseidon looked completely different. Instead of the serious man with cropped hair and simple toga, I found myself looking at a fierce tan-skinned man, with long white hair that should have aged him, but instead made him look dignified and extremely attractive. He was still wearing a toga, but I could swear it was made from the ocean itself, greens and blues and whites crashing together across the fabric in rolling waves. A gleaming silver trident shone in his fist, easily three feet taller than he was. I couldn't help gulping. This was a god who had made it clear he didn't like me, and today he looked like he did not want to be fucked with. Had he done that on purpose? I dragged my eyes from him, and found Hermes and Dionysus both grinning at me, and both wearing matching Hawaiian shirts with bright orange palm trees and parrots on them. A smirk leapt to my lips and they flashed me the thumbs up.

At the end of the row, and just as imposing as Hades' swirling smoke and Poseidon's glowing trident, was Zeus.

He seemed to have merged the pretty boy image from the coffee shop with the dark haired older man I'd also seen him as, and the result was quite breathtaking. He looked like a retired football player who hadn't stopped training, his muscles bulging and experienced confidence emanating from him. Even from where I was standing I could see the purple lightning in his eyes, and feel his infectious energy. Something in my blood responded to him, like it had with the rose throne. But instead of feeling drawn to him, I felt a heat that I was pretty sure wasn't passion. I didn't know what it was, but it made my body hum, and that restless sense of urgency crept through my muscles and made me fidget.

'And now, for the announcement of the next Trial,' boomed the commentator and every god but Poseidon sat down on their throne.

Oh shit.

'You may rise,' said the ocean god, his voice lyrical and strong. I stood up, glancing to each side of me at Hecate and Skop as nerves skittered through me. 'I have agreed to take some pressure off my dear brother's realm, and host the next Trial in Aquarius.' I looked at Hades. His smoke was rippling steadily. 'All I will tell you now is that you can expect to get wet,' Poseidon said, and I looked back at him to find his eyes locked on mine. I gave him an awkward smile and bowed my head. 'We will begin at midday tomorrow, and if you survive, I shall host a feast in your honor.

If I survive? Gods above, what did he have planned for me?

'I look forward to it,' I lied, wondering if he would be more likely to celebrate if I didn't make it.

'I'm sure,' he said, and I could hear the thinly veiled malice in his voice. What was his problem?

'Well, there you have it, folks! We'll see you tomorrow at midday for the next of Persephone's Trials!' the commentator said, and Poseidon sat back down as Dionysus rose.

'How's it going?' he said to the room at large, a wonky grin on his face and his dark hair screwed up in a bun on top of his head. 'I've sorted us out some entertainment, enjoy,' he said, and waved his hand in front of him. He looked every bit like a stoned seventies rock star, and each time I saw him I desperately wanted to hang out with him. The air shimmered a gorgeous green color, and then four impossibly tall girls appeared, wearing different colored little tutu skirts. A cheer went up from the crowd. As I looked closer I realized they all had pale tattoos covering their deep brown skin, of vines and flowers. A drum beat ricocheted through the room, making me start, then more drums began to beat along with the first. It was a tribal sound that both set me on edge and made me want to move at the same time, until a beautiful flute began to play over the top. A wave of happiness washed over me, and the four girls began to sway their hips in a synchronized dance. Slowly, the crowd began to chat again, some dancing too, some just staring at the girls.

'Dionysus's party dryads,' said Hecate at my side.

'They're very beautiful,' I said.

'Ohhh,' moaned Skop.

'You alright?' I asked him.

'*Not that hanging round with you all the time isn't fun, but this used to be my daily view,*' he said, staring at the four girls, his tail wagging furiously.

'Oh. Sorry,' I said. 'I can see why you would miss them. They're quite mesmerizing.'

'*Not as mesmerizing as you.*' The voice was in my head but it wasn't Skop's.

'Hades?' I whirled, and found him stood behind me, smoky and translucent. Everyone around him was giving him a wide berth, hushed and watching.

'Evening, boss,' said Hecate, then touched my shoulder. 'See you in a bit,' she said, and sashayed off into the crowd.

'*You look stunning tonight,*' Hades said, still inside my head.

'Thanks,' I replied, pleasure tingling through me at his words.

'*You should answer me silently, or tongues will wag.*'

'Fuck 'em. Let them hear one half of the conversation,' I said loudly. 'I'm not hosting or being judged today.'

My belligerent statement was rewarded with a flash of laughing silver eyes, and a glimpse of his soft lips in a broad smile. Heat pooled in my core. Those lips... Gods, I was like a randy teenager!

'*As you wish. I think you will like Aquarius. You used to love it.*'

'Well, I love swimming,' I told him.

'*That is good. Poseidon will not make this easy for you.*'

'Why does he hate me?'

'He does not hate you. He fears you.'

'What?'

'With all your power, you were a formidable goddess.'

Formidable? I would have liked the sound of that, if it didn't come with the knowledge that powerful Persephone had killed someone's wife.

'Well, I'm just little ol' human Persephone now, with only enough power to heal myself and survive your temper,' I shrugged. I got another flash of his face, this time pinched and serious.

'I wish you wouldn't remind me of that,' he said, voice low.

'Well, I wish you hadn't gone all monster and corpses on me, but we don't all get what we wish for.' I wasn't backing down on this. He deserved to feel bad for what he had done. And saying the words reminded me that as intoxicating as he was, I didn't belong here.

'I am a monster. I told you that.'

'Yes you did, but then you kissed me anyway,' I shot back. There was a collective gasp around us, and I scanned the onlookers as my cheeks heated. My eyes fell on one furious face in particular, and my stomach clenched. Minthe. And her glare was so loaded with venom I might have dropped down dead on the spot if looks could kill.

Hades chuckled in my mind.

'I told you we should have kept this conversation private.' I stood up straight, and flicked my loose curls dramatically over my shoulder. There was no way he was

winning this one. I would give them something to gossip about.

'Yes, Hades, I know being with me blew your mind and I know you cried like a baby afterward, but we're not doing it again. Now, please stop bothering me.'

I heard his deep, booming laugh in my head as I spun on my heels and marched away from him.

'Well played, Beautiful. Well played.'

SEVEN

PERSEPHONE

I f I had thought his voice was sexy, it was nothing compared to his laugh. Desire throbbed through me as I stomped blindly into the crowd. I wanted to listen to that laugh for the rest of my life. Longer, if possible. I wanted to be the cause of his laughter, to light up his face with that exquisite smile...

Gods, this was impossible! I screwed my face up and forced myself to look for someone I knew. Eros caught my eye and I changed direction immediately. The last thing my aching body needed was a conversation with the god of lust. The scent of salty sea air suddenly cascaded over me and my steps faltered as my head filled with images of endless, life-giving ocean. *What I wouldn't give to spend the day on the beach right now.*

'Hello, Persephone,' said a lyrical voice, and Poseidon shimmered into the space in front of me. I stopped, and bowed.

'Poseidon,' I said, my stomach flipping. How was it

that I now found the ocean god more scary than the King of the Underworld? I needed to revisit my priorities. 'I'm very much looking forward to seeing Aquarius. I've heard it's beautiful.'

'You've heard correctly. I want to offer you some advice.'

'Really?'

'Your powers were removed for a good reason. You would be wise to keep it that way. An ability to heal and feed plants is plenty enough. We both know that you will not win this competition.'

'How do you know that's all I can do?'

'Girl, I am one of the three strongest gods in Olympus,' he said, the waves now crashing across the material of his toga, a deep rumble building in his voice. 'There is nothing I don't know.' My heart began pounding in my chest as a primal fear crept over me.

'Right,' I whispered.

'My brother made his mistakes with you once already. I will not allow him to make them a second time.'

At his mention of Hades a defensiveness flashed up inside me out of nowhere, and I felt my face tighten into a scowl.

'Are you telling me you're trying to protect your brother, one of the *other* three most powerful gods in Olympus, from me? Seriously?'

'Watch your tongue!' he spat, and a gust of damp air lifted my hair from my shoulders. 'I have no personal grudge against you, Persephone, but I will do what needs to be done.'

'I didn't ask to be here!' I'd meant to put force into the words, but I hadn't meant them to come out as the shriek they did. It was like something had finally snapped inside me, the anger and frustration and injustice of everything that had happened breaking free from the fragile container I'd built around them. 'I was fucking kidnapped! From a life I loved! And now you're threatening me? Do you have any idea at all what you people have put me through?'

'You are the same,' Poseidon hissed, his eyes glowing an intense blue. 'Your wrath is no less as a human, your temper as hot and unpredictable as it ever was.'

'You'd lose your fucking temper if you'd had your memories and power stolen!' Rage was burning through my blood, heating my whole body, and sending almost painful tingles across my skin. 'Everyone is happy to talk about my past, but nobody will tell me what I did! I'm being forced to risk my life, and the lives of strangers and the only friends I have here, for your entertainment! And nobody even expects me to survive, let alone win! Do you understand that I am not here to make your life difficult? I don't want to be here!'

Something black burst from my hands as I threw them in the air angrily, and I stumbled backwards in shock. *Vines.* Black vines were curling from my palms, barbed and glowing.

'What the-' I started, but in a flash Hades was there, between me and Poseidon. The sea god grew, his trident pulsing with blue light, and Hades smoke flickered and danced outward, matching Poseidon's size.

'Goading her into losing her temper isn't very fair, brother,' said Hades calmly. I barely heard him over the rushing in my ears as I stared dumbly at the vines still coiling from my hands towards them.

'Stop,' I pleaded quietly, but they kept growing.

'You need to see that she is still a threat. You are blind to the danger she poses,' Poseidon said loudly.

'Zeus brought her here, not me. Go and take it up with him.' Black spots were creeping into my vision now, the vines almost reaching Hades.

'Fine. But you've not heard the last of this,' snapped Poseidon, then vanished.

'Shit, shit, shit,' muttered Hades the second he left, the smoke disappearing from around him as he turned to me. 'Persephone, you need to lose the vines, now.'

'I'm trying!'

'They'll go if you calm down, take deep breaths and think about something that doesn't make you angry.'

'Everything here makes me fucking angry!' I shouted, and the vines burst out further, curling around his feet. Frustration crossed his face as he pushed his hand through his hair, then the world flashed white.

When the light cleared, I instantly felt the surging rage inside me change; a brighter, optimistic feeling forcing it out of my veins. I was in the conservatory.

'Vent. Use your power, give it to the earth,' Hades said. I didn't need to ask him what he meant, his instruction felt like the most natural thing in the world. I flicked my wrists towards the closest flower bed, and the vine glowed as a vivid green color snaked over the black. It spread fast, turning the whole vine green in seconds. The end of the vines hit the soil, and a joyous feeling made my chest expand, the vines burrowing deeper.

I didn't know how long I stood there, channeling all my rage and pent up energy into the soil, but Hades said nothing the whole time. Eventually the vines melted away, and I felt a pang of loss as the blissful feeling faded. Being connected to the earth like that was more than incredible. It was as though I'd finally found a place I had always yearned for but didn't really know existed.

I turned to Hades and almost took a step back at the hunger evident on his face.

'You're beautiful,' he breathed.

'Erm, I just offended Poseidon, showed everyone I can't control my temper or power, and had some sort of out-of-body experience with a flowerbed. I fail to see the attraction just now,' I said on a long breath.

'When you use your power to grow things, to create life, you... You become practically irresistible.' He ground out the last word, like he really was struggling to resist something. *To resist me.*

'But... doesn't creating life kinda undermine what you do here?'

He let out a long breath.

'Yes. I have never understood it either.' A wave of exhaustion rocked over me before I could reply, and I stumbled, dizzy. Hades was there in an instant, his strong arms supporting me.

'You smell awesome,' I told him, my vision clouding. He tensed.

'Do you have any idea how hard it is not to rip your clothes off right now?' he hissed. 'I can't be this close to you.'

It was the last thing I heard him say, before I passed out.

EIGHT

PERSEPHONE

W hen I woke up I was in my bed, and Hades'
silver eyes were boring into my bleary ones.

'What happened?' I mumbled thickly.

'Your powers are returning. You lost your temper.'
The fight with Poseidon came back to me clearly, and
anxiety gripped my gut.

'Oh gods, that was in front of the whole room,' I
groaned, rubbing my hand across my face.

'Nobody but the gods saw. Remember how I can hide
us in smoke?'

'Yeah, the smoke bubble,' I said, remembering the
blissful stolen kiss in that haven he had created at the
ball.

'Well, Poseidon can make his own. He didn't want
anyone but me to see your exchange.'

'You said he fears me. Why?'

Hades blew out a long breath.

'Persephone, your powers and your wrath were... unique.'

A sick feeling crawled through me, and I didn't want to be having this conversation any more.

'Well, I only have a bit of my power now, and I don't intend on getting any more. I'm sure I'll stay perfectly harmless,' I said, pushing myself up to a sitting position. 'Where's Skop?'

'*On the floor. This asswipe won't let me on the bed,*' I heard his voice say in my head.

'You're not going to eat the other seeds?' Hades stared at me.

'No.' I dropped my gaze to my lap.

I hadn't been sure before, but now I was positive. There was no way I needed this dark, angry kind of power running through me. I knew it was part of a terrible past, and I needed to concentrate on the future.

'Persephone, look at me.' I lifted my head and did as he asked. His skin glowed and his eyes shone bright. He was *unfeasibly* beautiful. 'You must never be scared of your own strength,' he said quietly.

'I've never had any strength,' I answered him, unable to keep the bitter edge from my voice. 'I've let other people treat me like shit for years, because I've never had any strength.'

His jaw tightened, and fury flashed in his eyes, orange flames leaping then vanishing in his irises.

'They made me take your strength, when I sent you away. You were scared, and I wasn't allowed to fix it. I prayed the fear would leave you when you started again in the mortal world.' His words were hardly more than a whisper, but they carried a sorrow that was unbearable to hear. My hand went to his face automatically, the need to comfort him, to relieve this heart-breaking burden from him, overwhelming me.

'I got there in the end,' I told him. 'I learned, and I started to stand up for myself. In fact, until you lot showed up, I was doing pretty well.'

'There is a Queen inside you, Persephone. My Queen.'

Heat rushed me all at once, and there was nothing in the world that could feel better than hearing this man call me his queen. I sucked in a breath as I felt my cheeks burn.

'Well, I think I was starting to find her,' I said.

'I hope she stays with you when you get back.'

Physical pain seemed to blossom in my chest at his words, and I clawed about in my mind for the cause.

I wanted to leave. I wanted to go home. So why did it feel like he was betraying me by talking about sending me back?

'You still want me to leave?' I asked, before I could stop myself.

'I never wanted you to leave in the first place. But you can't stay here.'

I closed my eyes and flopped back onto the pillows. This was a conversation with no ending, just endless frustration. *Move on, Persephone.*

'Why did I pass out?' I asked him, opening my eyes.

'The power drained you. You'll need to make sure it doesn't happen in a more dangerous environment.'

'Like in the middle of a Trial?'

'Yes.'

'How?'

'You'll train with me from now on.'

'What?' I sat up again, eyebrows high.

'Every day. In combat and magic.'

I was going to see him every day? It was already getting hard to stop thinking about him all the time, how the hell was I going to stop myself from lusting after him if I spent *more* time with him? *Smoke and death, smoke and death!*

'Fine, but no magic sex,' I told him firmly. The corner of his mouth lifted.

'Agreed. No magic sex.' I shoved the disappointment that he'd agreed so readily deep down and nodded. 'Good,' he said. 'Now, get some rest before the Trial tomorrow. It's going to be tough.'

'OK. And... Thanks.'

'Always,' he said, and then he was gone.

I didn't visit the Atlas garden in my dreams that night. I wished I had, the calming, serene place was exactly what I needed, and the stranger often left me with more information than I'd had before visiting.

Instead, I dreamed of fire and blood. Screams filled my ears, until the roar of a beast began to drown them out. Then Hades burst through the flames, huge and monstrous and blue, his eyes burning with fury and everything around him turning to ash.

I woke up panting, fear making my heart hammer in my chest as I sat upright.

'You OK?' Skop asked, lifting his head from his paws. I nodded at him in the faint starlight coming from the ceiling. Since both Poseidon and Hades had flouted his guard duties, he had been extra protective the rest of the evening.

'Just a nightmare.'

'You want to talk to Morpheus about that,' he said, then settled back down.

There was no need for that, I thought, laying my head back down on my pillow. I knew exactly what the dream meant. It was my subconscious reminding me that Hades was dangerous.

I dressed in fighting garb the next day, and tied my hair up in a braid that kept it out of my face. If I was to be swimming, I didn't need my vision obscured by loose hair. I also left off the leather corset I normally wore over my shirt. It was heavy, and whilst it offered some protection from the blows of weapons, I was guessing that maneuverability would benefit me more in this Trial.

While I sat and waited for someone to come and get me, I stared at the open box of pomegranate seeds on the dresser. They pulled at me, and I thought about the black vines that had shot from my hands. *Strength.* They had felt strong and useful and deadly. I'd never had power like that at my disposal. Ted Hammond flashed into my mind, followed swiftly by an image of the black vines wrapping around his throat as he groped at me. An ugly, alien satisfaction filled me at the thought. *Stop it. You're not petty or vengeful,* I told myself sternly. I forced the image away, replacing it with the memory of when the vines had turned green, and that joyful feeling of being connected to the ground, of feeling the sparks of new life embedded in the earth. And that had just been in the starved conservatory. The idea of connecting like that with a real garden sent shudders of excitement through me.

I had my hand on the box before I'd even realized I'd moved.

'Woah there,' I scolded myself, jumping up from my stool and snapping the lid closed. 'I have *got* to get better at avoiding temptation.'

'You're doing a good job so far, you've managed to resist me,' said Skop.

'Gnome dogs really aren't my type,' I told him.

'I could try and change your mind?'

'Nope.'

'It was worth a shot.'

I was relieved when Hecate finally knocked on my door. The wait was making my nerves worse.

'You ready for this?' she asked, handing me her now customary gift of coffee. I took it gratefully.

'Nope. But water is better than heights or demons,' I said. 'And to be truthful, I'm excited to see Aquarius. Is it underwater?'

'Sure is. The city is spread across loads of underwater domes. It's pretty cool.'

'How do people get between them?'

'Tunnels. Or they swim. Lots of water nymphs and merfolk in Aquarius.'

'Merfolk? Like, actual mermaids?'

Hecate laughed and shook her head.

'There you go again, looking like a kid who has just had a wish granted. Honestly, you should see your face.'

'You try living in New York all your life and then finding out this is all real,' I retorted, and took a drag of my coffee. *Mermaids*. Gods I wanted to see one.

'You've seen a Spartae Skeleton, minotaurs, a freaking phoenix, and the gods know what besides. Why are merfolk a big deal?'

'I don't know,' I lied. I'd be damned before admitting my deep-rooted love for children's animated movies to her.

'Weirdo. Finish that up, we need to go.'

The room she flashed us into followed a pattern, I realized as I stared around it. I knew it was a throne room immediately, and not just because of the dais covered in huge seats, but because, like Hades' throne room and Zeus' dining room, there were no walls, just riveted columns holding up the ceiling. But the view here...

Turquoise-blue water surrounded us completely, and beyond I could see hundreds of glowing gold domes. Floating at different levels, they were all connected by tunnels, and I could just make out buildings inside most of them, colored white and bronze. In the distance, behind the city, I could see a pod of massive whales meandering past.

It was stunning.

I was standing on a marble floor that at first I thought was white, but when the rays of light filtering through the water hit it, looked the palest blue. The ceiling was painted with the most incredible underwater scene I could imagine, pastel corals hiding hundreds of brightly colored fish, and images of creatures that looked like they had come from another planet surrounding them. The empty thrones were all plain, except the one in the center, which was shaped like a tidal wave, smooth and fierce and perfect.

'Wow,' I breathed.

'I know. Grumpy he may be, but Poseidon has taste,' Hecate said quietly.

'I appreciate that,' boomed Poseidon's voice, and Hecate winced.

'Shit.'

The twelve gods flashed onto the dais, and when the light cleared I saw the commentator standing in front of them, his white toga as crisp as his smile.

'Good day Olympus!'

I looked straight to Hades, his smoke rippling. A flash of silver in the darkness found my eyes and I suppressed my shiver of delight. *Gods, I was getting worse.* 'Welcome to Aquarius! I'll waste no time in handing you over to your host.'

Hecate bowed low, and I followed suit as Poseidon stepped forward, and the other gods lowered themselves into their seats. The sea god looked as he had the previous night, trident resplendent as it towered above him.

'I have devised a test fit for the Queen of an Olympian. You must get the gem back in the trident. You must complete the trial alone. Other than that there are no rules.'

Put a gem in a trident. That didn't sound too bad, I thought, trying to ignore the bit about a test fit for a Queen. And at least I knew what I had to do this time. No running around guessing and trying to decipher stupid clues.

'You will be granted the temporary ability to breath underwater, and a steed,' Poseidon continued, and my mouth dropped open.

Say what? Breathing underwater and a freaking steed?

'But by no means will you be immune to any other dangers of the ocean. Understood?'

'Erm,' I said, but he banged his trident on the floor before I could say any more.

'Let us begin!'

NINE

PERSEPHONE

I gasped as cold water enveloped me, the world turning upside down as my feet were swept out from under me. The sound of rushing water drowned out my yell, and I tumbled over and over as waves crashed all around me. Instinct made me clamp my mouth shut as I inhaled a mouthful of salty water, then I was completely submerged. The light dimmed and panic and disorientation gripped me. I kicked out, feeling for the floor or anything solid, unable to see. My lungs were burning as I flailed my limbs desperately. Then the swirling motion flinging my body about stopped abruptly, and bright light began to seep back through the water. I tried to steady myself, treading water, chest aching as I looked around.

I was at the bottom of the ocean.

Directly ahead of me was a huge sunken marble trident, jutting out of the sandy ocean-bed, its three points stabbing majestically towards the surface. I started to turn to look for more but dizziness made my eyes roll. I needed air.

'Breathe. You can breathe under here.'

'Hades!'

'Breathe.'

Gods, this was messed up. I closed my eyes, and forced out every instinct in my body screaming at me to keep my mouth shut.

I inhaled.

Instead of water, cool air filled my throat, then my lungs, and I laughed aloud in relief as my eyes fluttered open. *I was breathing underwater.* Unreal. I kicked myself around in a slow circle, taking in everything I could.

To the right of the fifty-foot tall trident, high up and floating on a platform, were the twelve gods, and a little way apart from them, the three judges. I threw a pointed scowl at them all, and moved my gaze on.

The ocean bed was littered with ruined buildings, white marble and lumps of bronze nestled in the sand. Only one structure looked like it had survived whatever had sunk it, but it wasn't in good shape. I guessed the gem that I had to hunt out and put in the trident would be hidden down there. I was quite sure there would be more to it than just finding it though. A treasure hunt wasn't exactly perilous enough for these sadistic bastards.

Didn't Poseidon say something about a steed? As soon as the thought entered my mind, my legs began to feel tired. With a final glance at the gods, I kicked myself down, swimming towards the intact building. There was no point tiring myself out treading water and achieving nothing.

The water was cool but not cold, and it felt good to be swimming. I'd swum in pools all my life, but swimming in the sea was a luxury I could seldom afford while living in Manhattan. I was glad I'd left the leather corset off, my arms pulling me easily through the water.

As I reached the entrance to the building, the hairs on my arms stood up and I slowed. It looked like I would expect an ancient Greek temple to look, with a triangular facade topping cracked columns. It was single story, and half of it seemed to have sunk into the sand, leaving it severely lop-sided. I peered through the columns into the darkness.

Something rushed at me from the gloom, and I shot backwards, drawing *Faesforos* from the sheath on my thigh instinctively. But as I saw the thing, my knife arm dropped to my side limply, and my jaw dropped.

It was a seahorse. And not the kind of seahorse that I'd seen in aquariums back home, but an actual horse, with a fish's tail curled underneath him instead of back legs. In place of hair he had a solid covering of tiny irides-cent scales that shone and caught the light like mother-of-pearl, and he rocked and whinnied as he bounded in circles around me. Unbridled joy filled me as I watched him, and I felt like a child falling in love with ponies again.

'*It's a hippocampus. They're not the most intelligent creatures, but tame enough,*' said Hades voice in my head.

'Are you allowed to talk to me?'

As soon as I projected the thought to him, a hot swell of water lifted me, and Poseidon's voice echoed in my head.

'Enough help!'

I'll take that as a no then, I thought, and reached a hand out hesitantly to the hippocampus. He bumped his large, cold nose against my hand and gave a gleeful little whinny. A smile split my face, and I noticed a simple strap over his back, with a stirrup on either side. I swam up and over him, and he stayed perfectly still in the water as I maneuvered my feet into the stirrups. I couldn't see how the strap was staying fixed to his back, so I guessed magic was involved. The cold scales weren't as comfortable as a saddle would have been, but this would definitely beat swimming. I tried to ignore the creeping worry that I might be down here some time if they expected me to need to ride this fella to keep going.

As soon as I set my sights on the ruined building again, a deep rumbling started beneath me, and the hippocampus kicked in alarm.

'Easy, buddy,' I said, soothing his neck and looking down. The sand in the clearing in the center of the building was vibrating, dust clouds lifting into the water. 'Let's not wait and find out what that is, eh?' I said to the hippocampus, adrenaline beginning to surge though my veins. Something bad was coming, I knew it. The hippocampus made a loud clicking sound in response. 'How do I make you go forward?'

My words were lost to the water around me, only audible as a bubbly mess of noise to me, but it seemed my steed understood them perfectly. He darted forward, and I gripped his neck in surprise at his speed, then squeaked in alarm as I realized he wasn't slowing down. 'Slow down!' He did, immediately, and I let out a long breath, bubbles rising around my face. 'Left a bit?' I asked him tentatively, and the rumbling grew louder. He swerved left. Good. 'And right?' He changed course, heading right. 'Excellent,' I told him. 'Let's go get this gem.'

I couldn't help glancing over my shoulder as we charged towards the gloom of the temple.

I wished I hadn't.

The sand in the clearing was beginning to churn, and I could just make out giant black claws peeking up through the ground, tips sharp and lethal looking. If whatever it was had claws bigger than me, I shuddered to think how huge the rest of it was.

I snapped my attention back to the job at hand as we zoomed between two columns, and into the temple.

'Slow down a bit, buddy,' I said, straining to see in the darkness. The hippocampus did slow down, but he also made a funny squeaking sound, before beginning to glow. A soft blue light started emanating from him, casting just enough illumination about us for me to make out more columns and what was left of a cracked marble floor, sinking into the ground. Something large scuttled on my right, and I jumped in surprise.

Trying not to think about what else might be in there with me, I urged the hippocampus on. 'That's a neat trick.

I'm going to have to give you a name,' I told him, as we floated cautiously through the room, me scanning the ground beneath us for anything that looked like a gem. 'How about Buddy? I keep calling you that anyway.' He snickered and I nodded. 'Buddy it is.' A loud screech from outside the temple carried through the water to me, and I shivered. We needed to do this faster.

We did a full circuit of the room, finding nothing but more broken rock and marble, and lots and lots of large crabs. I grimaced as I realized we were going to have to go further into the temple. There were two dark doorways at the back of the room and we hovered before them. Choosing the one on the left arbitrarily, I directed Buddy towards it, and we swam through.

It was pitch black, and Buddy's soft glow failed to penetrate the darkness. A primal fear of not knowing what was in the dark crawled over my skin. Heat swept over me as I blinked and I realized that being completely submerged in water was a much, much more suffocating feeling when the water wasn't nice and cool. A budding panic started to blossom in my chest as Buddy turned in a slow circle, and the water around me heated more. Despite every breath I took being dry air, my lungs were straining, and it felt like I couldn't fill them enough. Tightness was spreading across my whole chest now, and I knew the signs of oncoming panic in my body too well. Big black spots would come soon, along with the dizziness.

'We'll come back to this room,' I said, even my blurry underwater voice sounding breathless. Buddy seemed to agree, wasting no time at all speeding back to the doorway. The gloom of the main hall seemed positively bright compared to the dark room, and the water we moved through was mercifully cool, almost like a balm over my skin. I took long breaths as Buddy slowed, petting his neck absent-mindedly as I reassessed the hall, my racing pulse calming. 'Let's hope the gem is in the other room,' I said to him. ''Cos I do not want to go back in there. Ever.'

The ceiling in the second room was cracked, and the gaps were letting in shafts of blue light that shimmered over an array of rotting wooden crates. We were on the raised side of the building, the side that wasn't sinking, and I couldn't have been more grateful for the extra light.

'OK. Let's see what we've got,' I said nervously, and slid my feet from Buddy's stirrups. Swallowing my trepidation, I kicked myself over to the nearest crate and reached for the lid. I'd half expected the wood to crumble under my touch, but it felt sturdy as I eased the lid up. There was no hinge, and the lid slid off, hitting the sandy marble and causing a wave of dust to lift from the floor. I heard a distinct slithering sound and froze, trying to tread water as gently as I could while looking slowly around myself for the source of the sound. Nothing was moving though, and I let out a long breath as I swam over the top of the open box to look inside.

Books. Piles and piles of books, probably submerged

in water for centuries. I felt a pang of sorrow that they were ruined, then another distant screech made me focus. I needed to check the next box.

I went through them all and whilst I found some pretty awesome stuff, none of it was a gem. There was an unbelievably sharp looking sword, a large box full of rusted armor, and a whole host of cooking paraphernalia, but nothing that looked like treasure. Swimming back over the top of the boxes towards Buddy, I sighed. 'Guess we'd better go back to the room of panic,' I told him, then froze.

Wrapping itself tightly around the first crate I'd opened was a snake. An enormous freaking sea snake. Documentaries I'd seen about how reptiles flashed bright colors as a warning to other animals popped into my head as I stared at it. This thing was neon-bright, don't-fuck-with-me orange. It was also massive, looping itself three times around the box already, with more tail seeming to come from nowhere. And it was between me and the doorway and my hippocampus.

Would it care if I just swam over it, or would it attack? A thought stopped me from kicking up higher and trying though. What if it was wrapped round that partic-ular box for a reason? Was there such a thing as a guard snake? *But that box was full of books, not gems.* Although... I hadn't removed any of the books. Or looked underneath them.

Pulse racing, I swam back to the box with the sword in it, and hefted it up out of the crate. It weighed a ton and I screwed my face up, dropping it again immediately.

There was no way I could wield it. Besides which, I didn't really want to kill or piss off the snake. Just get it to move out of the way. I began to dig through the crates, tossing things out as I hunted for something that might distract the serpent. It didn't move from the box of books, but its head lifted warily, beady black eyes fixed on me as I launched bits of ancient sunken trash through the water.

My eyes fell on the rusted armor, a new plan forming quickly in my head as yet another screech from outside reverberated through the building. I reached into the box and lifted out a dented shield with a sun carved on it. It was heavy, but nowhere near as bad as the sword, and it seemed solid enough. I fought with the straps on the inside, eventually looping my left forearm through so I was wearing it properly. It was large enough that when I held my arm in front of me it covered my whole body, down to the waist. It wasn't ideal, but it was the best I had. It would have to do.

'Here we go,' I told Buddy, and swam towards the snake and the box of books.

TEN

PERSEPHONE

The snake's head reared back as I got close and it hissed, a purple forked tongue flicking from its mouth. A frisson of fear skittered through me but I swam on, covering myself with the rusted shield. I swam high over the snake, staying well out of reach of its head as I got over the top of the box. I squinted down, scanning for anything that looked out of place and my gaze snagged on a leather-bound book that had a bright orange cover, just visible under a few of the others. *Orange like the snake.* Was that a clue?

Steeling myself, I focused on the book and tipped my body in the water, so that I was pointing head-first at the box. Raising the shield I took a deep breath, and darted downward.

The snake went for me the second I was within its range, hitting the shield with such force that I rolled hard through the water. Gasping, I tried to angle myself down, sending a million silent thanks to the gods that the ancient shield had held. I felt water swoosh past me as I frantically reached into the box, lifting my shield arm around my back to protect myself. Shoving other books aside, I managed to close my fingers around the bound edge of the orange book just before something slammed into the back of my legs. I crashed hard into the crate, hitting my chin on a mercifully squishy book, the impact of the shield hitting the wooden sides of the box sending shockwaves through my arm. I rolled as best I could, still clutching the book, and saw the end of the snake's glowing tail coming for me just in time to bring the shield around to block it. There was another hissing sound, and adrenaline sent a surge of strength through my legs. I tucked them under myself and pushed hard against the side of the box, launching myself up and out of reach of the snake.

I wasn't fast enough though. I felt searing hot pain in my ankle as I kicked furiously, and looked down to see the creatures jaws wide open beneath me, red blood on the end of one of its fangs. *My blood.*

Praying it wasn't a venomous snake, I bolted towards the door and Buddy, trying to shake the heavy shield off my arm as my heart hammered in my chest.

'Let's go!' I called to the hippocampus as I shot straight past his rocking body, back through the doorway and as far away from the hissing neon snake as I could get. Once I was back in the gloomy main hall, I whirled, raising the shield still stuck on my arm, but mercifully only Buddy had followed me out of the room.

Grimacing, I managed to get my arm free from the

shield straps and gripped the book with both hands, treading water and trying to ignore the pain spreading up my calf. If this was just a normal, boring book I was going to lose my shit.

I opened it, holding my breath.

There, glowing bright with every color of the ocean, was a wide, flat gem, nestled in a hollow cut out of the book's pages. Relief washed through me, and I grabbed it triumphantly, dropping the book onto the floor. 'Nailed it,' I told Buddy, allowing myself a smile as I held up the gorgeous stone to show him. A pulse of pain from my leg transformed my smile swiftly into a scowl though. I lifted my knee to my chest in the water and twisted my leg, so that I could get a good look at the wound the snake had given me. It was a small cut, but it was shining with blood and was giving off a faint orange glow.

Shit. That did not look normal. I could heal though, right? As I tried to feel for my powers a wave of fatigue came over me, and I didn't know if it was from my physical encounter with the snake, or something worse. Like venom.

Putting the gem carefully into my pocket I kicked myself over to Buddy and wrestled my feet into his stirrups. It felt good to rest my legs as I sat down on his cold back, and I sagged a little, the adrenaline from both the terrifying pitch black room and my face off with the snake starting to ebb away.

'Let's see if I can use these damn powers,' I muttered, and closed my eyes, concentrating on the feeling I'd had in the conservatory.

After a full minute of trying, all I could feel was a pathetic tingle somewhere in my chest, and I was fairly certain I wasn't healing myself. My ankle still throbbed painfully. 'Fine. I give up. Let's get this over with,' I snapped, opening my eyes and patting Buddy on the neck. We bobbed together in the water as he whinnied. The best thing I could do was to finish the Trial, then get help. A piercing screech from outside echoed through the chamber and I gritted my teeth, feeling my pulse spike as I mentally geared up for what was coming next. 'Alright, alright, I'm going!' I yelled and directed Buddy towards the cracked columns at the front of the temple, and whatever it was that making that awful sound.

'Shit. Shit, shit, shit,' I breathed as we left the sinking building and emerged into the bright blue ocean.

The thing between me and the trident statue made the sea snake look positively tame.

My skin crawled as I stared, every part of my mind telling me to turn and run, and for the sake of the gods, don't turn back. The center of the clearing was now a swirling mass of sand, as though there was a whirlpool embedded into the ocean floor. And emerging from it like some sort of worm from a hole was the most hideous creature I'd ever seen. It was the same shape and color as a worm, but it was as wide as a house, and its head... Its whole head was a mouth. Needle-sharp teeth ringed its circular jaw, and huge claw-like black horns circled the outside of its head. Its skin was repulsive looking, cracked and rotten and leathery, and big drops of something the color of blood flicked out from it as it rolled and flailed through the water. It was about twenty feet out of the churning sand and I realized as the hippocampus reared back suddenly, that I was only just out of its reach.

'Now you face Charybdis!' boomed Poseidon's voice, and the creature screeched on hearing its name.

A surge of adrenaline wiped away the pain from my leg and the initial paralysis at seeing something so alien. My vision focused sharply, and I reached down to Buddy, who was vibrating with fear beneath me.

'I need your help, Buddy. We're way faster than this thing,' I told him, loading my voice with a confidence I prayed I could back up. 'But we need to go right now, before that thing gets out any further out of the sand. Go!'

The hippocampus burst to life, zooming up and over Charybdis so fast I could feel the skin on my face pulling against the force of the water. I glanced down as we soared over the monster, a flurry of excitement building inside me. We were doing it. We would reach the trident statue in no time.

But my breath caught and the excitement sank like a stone to the pit of my stomach the very next second. The thing was dropping back down into its hole, its massive round mouth forming the epicenter of the sand-whirlpool below me, and a jet of water blasted up from it, slamming into us and freezing Buddy's progress completely. He squealed beneath me, and panic flooded my system as I looked down and saw a second layer of razor sharp of teeth slice out under Charybdis' first set, jagged and stained and as big as I was. We were trapped in the beam of water, and like quicksand, it was sucking us downward.

'You can do it!' I urged the hippocampus, my heart hammering as I looked up at the trident statue. But he couldn't. Slowly and inexorably, we were being dragged towards the creature's terrifying maw.

I looked desperately between the trident and Charybdis, sand and ocean water swirling faster and faster around us. Buddy was moving backwards now, his frantic tail unable to keep beating at such a fast pace against the mighty pull of the monster. I felt utterly useless sat on his back, but if he couldn't break free of the whirlpool's force, there was no way I could.

I needed to do something else. Something that wasn't swimming. Whatever it was that I did best.

I fixed my sights on the center spike of the trident, and concentrated hard on Poseidon. I thought of what he had said to me, how he blamed me for being here, for posing a threat to Olympus. I thought about the way Eris had treated me at the masquerade ball, patronizing and cruel. I thought about Zeus, and his fucked up, inflated sense of entitlement and the shit he was putting Hades through.

Black vines burst from my palms, and a feeling like electricity burned through my entire body. There was no fear this time, no terror of what was happening. This time

I was in control. This time I *wanted* the vines. I launched them at the trident, bone-deep strength filling my body to the brim as I sent them snaking further through the water to wrap around the central spike.

Buddy squealed again and I snapped my attention down, dimly noticing that my arms were glowing green.

We were too close.

Charybdis was only ten feet below us, and a tremor of fear shuddered through my new found strength as I looked down past those insanely sharp teeth, into the black, rotten gullet of the beast.

No fucking way was I going down there.

I pulled hard on the vines, willing them to hold, willing them to be stronger than the whirlpool.

They were.

I cried out in pain as my wrists were yanked up hard, both of them making an awful snapping sound as we shot up through the sea. I squeezed my legs tightly around Buddy as we were dragged higher, tears streaming from eyes I couldn't keep open against the powerful flow of water. I didn't see the trident until it was too late, Buddy and I slamming into the cold marble. The pain in my wrists was so excruciating that I hardly noticed though, and I struggled to get my bearings as I belatedly realized we had come to a stop. I heard that hideous screech again and shook my head, blinking. Buddy tipped me forward with a whinny, so that I was looking down, and through my haze I saw Charybdis launching himself up from his hole.

The sight was all I needed to snap back into action. I

shoved my hand into my pocket, noticing first that the vines had gone, then yelling involuntarily at the pain. Gasping through the agony, I withdrew the gem. I had seconds before the beast reached us.

'Go!' I urged the hippocampus, and we pelted up, towards the tip of the central spike, the only one missing a gleaming blue gem. Heat engulfed us and I knew it was Charybdis' rotten breath as the light around us faded. His huge teeth moved into my peripheral vision as he reached us, and adrenaline flooded my body.

This was it. Now or never.

I screamed as I launched myself up from Buddy's back and slammed the gem into the empty recess, and the ring of teeth began to close around us.

ELEVEN

PERSEPHONE

The blood-stained teeth were barely a foot from us when white light flashed. For the first time since coming to this damned forsaken place, I couldn't have been more grateful for that light. It meant I was being transported somewhere else, and there was literally nowhere at that moment that could be worse.

I found myself on Poseidon's throne room floor again, dry and on my ass. I moved to stand as the light cleared from my vision, but immediately dropped back to the stone floor. My leg...

The wound on my ankle was turning black, the torn leather of my pants revealing how swollen it was. As I reached out to touch it new fear and pain blazed through me. I couldn't move my hands, and pain was lancing up my arms from my wrists with such intensity I could barely focus on anything else.

'You used the wrong gem,' boomed Poseidon, and I blinked up at him. He was standing in front of his throne, the eleven other gods behind him, just as they had been before I'd started the Trial. His face was different some-how, like he was straining against something.

'Where's Buddy?' I asked, before I could stop myself. Poseidon inclined his head a touch. 'The way you treated my hippocampus was commendable. He is safe.'

'Good. What do you mean I used the wrong gem?' I said through clenched teeth, trying to flex my fingers. Nothing but pain, shooting up my forearms. I felt sick.

'That gem was not the same as the other two in the trident. They were turquoise and the one you found was blue. The correct gem was in the other room. You may now be judged.'

My mouth fell open, but as I started to argue I was cut off.

'And so to the judges!' the commentator's voice sang out from behind me. I swiveled around on my butt, not giving a shit how it made me look. I couldn't stand, and I couldn't use my hands. Standing and falling on my face would look a lot worse. My head swam as I looked at the judges, fresh waves of pain stabbing through me. 'Radamanthus?'

'No tokens,' the cheerful judge smiled at me. I felt the fury morphing my face.

'Aeacus?'

'No tokens,' the serious man said.

'Minos?'

'No tokens.'

I glared at them as they vanished, injustice pounding through me, then the world flashed white once more.

. . .

I wasn't in my own room when the light faded. I was on a bed though, and I looked around warily, anger still rolling through me in waves, every pulse of pain tearing through my arms and leg making it worse.

I got past a snake and that freaking sea monster and got nothing at all for it? This was complete and total bull-shit! *You don't want to win, what the hell are you angry about?* The rational voice inside me cut through the fury. And it was right. I didn't want to win, I just wanted to survive. This was a good outcome.

But it didn't feel good. In fact, I didn't feel good.

A fuzzy feeling overcame me as I tried to take in my surroundings, and my vision abruptly turned bleary.

'Is she alright?' said an urgent male voice, and I tried to look for the source but instead felt the top half of my body collapsing on the pillows behind me.

'I don't know, get out of the damned way!' answered a female voice that my brain barely registered as Hecate's, before I blacked out completely.

'You know, you should stop passing out after every Trial. It's not a great look.'

I sat up quickly, and Hecate leaped backwards before I accidentally head-butted her.

'My hands!' I said, fear making my skin crawl. I hadn't been able to use my hands... I raised them fast, and watched my fingers flex in relief. They were working, and they didn't hurt at all.

'They're fine now. Your vines broke both your wrists, that's all.'

I looked at her incredulously.

'*That's all?* Are you serious?'

'Yeah I'm serious. You just needed a rest to fix those, the venom in your ankle was a totally different story. That shit nearly killed you.'

'R-really?'

'Yeah. Good job one of the most powerful gods in the world has a soft spot for you,' she said, with a little wink.

'Hades?'

'He healed you. He'll get in some serious shit if anyone finds out, but to be honest I'm not sure what else Zeus can do to him.' She sighed and sat down on the edge of my bed. It was narrow and I looked around as I processed her words. *Hades had healed me.*

'Where am I?'

'Infirmary.'

I nodded. That explained the metal cabinets lining the walls and the three other single beds.

'Where's Skop?'

'Hades wouldn't let him in here. Doesn't want Dionysus to know he healed you.'

'So... Are the other gods expecting me to die from the snake venom?' I asked. My tummy rumbled loudly. I was freaking ravenous.

'Nah, he'll make up some story about an apothecary

having the right antidote. Which will exist somewhere, but we didn't have time to find it.'

'Thanks. Again. For saving me.'

'I did nothing. This one was all up to the boss,' she said, but the smile she gave me was as real as any I'd seen. 'I know you're not gonna like this, but we have to go to Poseidon's party.'

'You're fucking kidding.' My stomach twisted as I stared at her. I needed some time to get over the fact that I apparently almost died. Again.

'I'm not. He told the world publicly that if you survived he would host a feast in your honor. So that's what he's doing, and you have to be there.'

'I got no damned tokens! I failed!'

'But you did survive. So get dressed.'

Hecate gave me a long yellow dress to wear, which was fairly plain except for the white daisies that adorned the skirt. I accepted her offer to magic my make-up and hair into something presentable, and sat still while her eyes glowed milky white opposite me.

This was ludicrous. They would have let me die for this damned competition. And they tricked me with a fucking fake gem. I mean, seriously, who would have noticed that it was a slightly different color? *Anyone who took the time to look properly,* answered the critical voice inside me that I'd spent years trying to squash. I felt my eyes narrow as I huffed.

'They're a bunch of fuckwits,' I announced, and the white leaked away from Hecate's eyes.

'Yup. You're all done.' There was no mirror to hand, but I trusted her. She'd made me look great before. 'Except Hades,' she added, moving to the door. 'He's less of a fuckwit than most of the others.' A thrill danced across my skin at hearing his name and I stopped myself from rolling my eyes. I needed to get over this. Now.

I followed Hecate through the door into a long corridor lit with torches. They burned a normal orange color, no blue fire, like the Underworld.

'Did you know it was the wrong gem?' I asked Hecate, unable to shift the anger I still felt about being duped.

'Well, it was pretty obvious that you had to get something from the dark room. The other one was too easy.'

'Easy?' I stopped in my tracks, eyebrows raised as high as they would go. 'Easy? That snake nearly killed me!'

'Yeah but the dark room was so bad you couldn't stand it for more than a minute. It was obviously the worse of the two.' I resumed my stride down the corridor, almost stamping after her, my fists clenched.

'This place is bullshit,' I seethed.

'So you keep saying. You know, you might end up offending some of the inhabitants if you carry on like this.'

'Most of the inhabitants are dickheads,' I snapped.

'I'm gonna take it you don't mean me,' Hecate answered slowly, blue light flickering around her dangerously. A trickle of alarm ran through my anger.

'No! Gods no, of course not.'

'Good. Although I *can* be a total bitch,' she said, with a small shrug as her blue light faded.

I didn't doubt it.

At the end of the corridor was a short flight of stairs leading down, and when we reached the bottom my rage abruptly abated as I took in where we were.

We were entering one of the tunnels I had seen earlier that connected the domes of Aquarius. And it was truly breathtaking.

The whole tunnel was clear, offering an unhindered view of the glowing gold domes all around us. I could see much more clearly what was inside the closest one now; white and bronze buildings surrounding a bustling court-yard filled with stalls. Most of the people I could make out were humans and they were wearing Asian style clothing, brightly colored saris and fabric everywhere.

'Aquarius is famous for jewelry markets,' Hecate said, stopping to let me stand and stare. 'We're on the east side, which is the shopping district. The west side of the city is more formal, all meeting halls and grand temples. And in the north the domes get bigger and more sparse because they're all farms.'

'Farms?'

'Yeah. Poseidon likes to be self-sustaining down here, so he has farms. I don't know how much of his power it uses growing stuff down here, but that's what he does. He doesn't trust the other gods.'

'He doesn't trust me either,' I mumbled, staring

through the water at the beautiful underwater city. 'Why is he so moody?'

'I'm guessing being Zeus' brother will do that to anyone after an eternity. Hades-' she started, but stopped. I turned to her and she bit down on her lip.

'Go on...'

'Hades deals with Zeus in a different way,' she said slowly. 'And he has more reason to dislike Zeus than Poseidon ever has.'

'Why?'

Hecate sighed.

'It really should be Hades telling you this,' she said, but continued. 'When Zeus rescued his siblings from Cronos and led the war against the Titans he became Lord of the Gods by default. And when handing out almighty roles in the new world, he made sure he became ruler of the Skies. The two most powerful remaining realms he gave to his brothers. The Ocean and the Underworld. One a place of life-giving, flowing power, the other a place of dark and terrifying misery.'

'Hades didn't choose to be King of the Underworld?' I breathed. Hecate shook her head sadly.

'No. He didn't. Zeus made the decisions. The three brothers took on the epic powers required of them to rule their domains. Poseidon gained ultimate control of water, Zeus of storms and sky and Hades... He is not a god of death. Thanatos is the god of death. But Hades was forced to become the only thing that could rule over and control the kingdom of the dead.'

'A monster,' I whispered, the hairs on my arms standing on end.

'Yes. He had to become more feared than any other god. It's not just the dead that reside in the Underworld, it's also home to the world's most dangerous gods and monsters, who have been trapped in Tartarus. If they or the dead rose... Olympus would fall.'

My mind was spinning as I tried to imagine a Hades who wasn't surrounded by smoke and death, a Hades who ruled the seas or the skies instead of the Underworld. Would he be different? Hell, I hardly knew anything about him now, how would I even know? And it wasn't like Zeus and Poseidon weren't terrifying in their own right. To an extent, they were all monsters.

'So, does he hate his brothers?' I asked. Was he an outcast? Memories of crying in my bunk in my parents' trailer flickered through my mind unbidden. I knew how it felt to be an outcast. I knew how differently people treated you.

'You'd have to ask him that. I certainly wouldn't call them friends. But Hades isn't stupid. Over the years he's aligned himself with the few beings in this world stronger than Zeus.'

'Oceanus?' I said, remembering what Skop had told me about Zeus being pissed that the ocean god was back.

Hecate looked at me in surprise.

'Yes. How'd you know that?'

'Skop. Oceanus is a Titan, right? Like you?'

'Yeah, except like a bazillion times more powerful than me. He, Prometheus, Atlas, Nyx, Helios, and a bunch of other Titans stayed neutral in the war. They mostly keep a low profile or have vanished though. Zeus despises Titans. But Oceanus returned recently.'

'So how come he hasn't taken the sea back from Poseidon?'

'It doesn't work like that,' Hecate said, and began walking down the tunnel. I followed after her. 'Poseidon rules this realm, not all the oceans. Sure, he has power over water, but he doesn't own it. Hephaestus' realm is under the sea too, made up of huge volcanic forges.'

'Oh. Can a god have more than one realm?'

'Funny you should mention that,' she said. 'No.' I waited for her to go on, but she stayed silent, our sandals on the glass tunnel the only sound.

'Why is it funny?' I prompted eventually.

'Talk to Hades about it. I'm sure you'll understand it better coming from him.' I rolled my eyes, but the truth was that I was secretly longing for any excuse to talk to him.

TWELVE

HADES

Why was she not here yet? The last time I had seen her, Persephone had been as white as the marble beneath my feet, the black poison from that cursed snake most of the way up her leg. Even with the ability to go anywhere instantly, I hadn't dared try to find the antidote. I hadn't known how much longer she had before the venom reached her heart, and then it would be too late.

Dread coiled its way through my chest at the thought of her death. This is why she was sent away! This was why I'd ripped a part of my soul out - to keep her safe. And now, here she was, at death's door every other damned day.

I realized the temperature was rising and took a slow breath, calming myself. Poseidon was acting cagey since the Trial, and I hadn't seen Zeus yet. Both would goad me tonight, I was sure. I needed a better handle on my temper. *I needed to see Persephone, alive and glowing and healthy.*

The feast in her honor was being held in the courtyard of a small dome, and it was decorated beautifully. A huge circular pool filled the middle of the pale brick ground, and female merfolk and ocean sprites splashed and played and batted their eyelashes at the other guests. Not that anyone was looking at merfolk's faces; they were all as naked as the day they were born. I barely noticed them as I scanned the dome yet again. Many lesser gods were present, talking and laughing under twinkling golden lights, the blue of the ocean casting a favorable light over them.

'She'll be here soon, Hades,' I heard Hera say in my mind. I looked sideways down the row of thrones at her, but her gaze was fixed on the crowd.

'I know,' I answered gruffly.

'I spoke with her, you know. After the masquerade ball.' My heart skipped a beat. 'She is an enigma. So much of your fierce Queen has been buried too deep to resurrect.' I thought of Persephone's own words, and anger and pain gripped me. *I've let other people treat me like shit for years, because I've never had any strength.* I'd done that to her. She had been one of the strongest women I'd ever known, and I'd left her defenseless and alone.

'She will not be in Olympus long,' I said to Hera,

forcing my emotions down. This was the way it had to be. I had already accepted that twenty-six years ago.

'I wouldn't be so sure about that. Strength born from overcoming trauma is very different to blood-born arrogance. It is true strength.'

'What?'

'Her experience as a human has changed her. Instead of being born to power, she's had to earn it. And the more we put her through, the stronger she may become. Stronger even than she was before.'

'No,' I snapped, but conflicting feelings of excitement and fear rippled through me. Stronger than she was before? Was Poseidon right to fear her? But imagine her with true power, ruling by my side...

My body responded immediately to the vision blossoming in my mind. Persephone on the Rose throne, resplendent in one of her fierce black corseted gowns, an onyx crown atop her head and black vines coiling from her palms as she glowed with power. Arousal throbbed through me.

She walked into the dome at that exact second and she couldn't have looked less like the woman I was imagining.

She was wearing a yellow dress, with white daisies on it, and she was wide-eyed with awe. She looked delicate and young and vibrant and innocent and... *And I wanted her even more.*

Her eyes found me almost immediately, and a bolt of something deeper than desire tore through me. I couldn't handle it. All my resolve to avoid her and merely lust after her from afar disintegrated, and I was standing in front of her within a second.

'Oh! Hello,' she said, and I could hear the nerves in her voice. Was she still afraid of me?

'Hello. I'm glad to see you looking so... healthy.'

'I hear you are to thank for that,' she said. I could see her eyes scanning my smoky exterior, and I deliberately dropped it from my face just long enough to let her see me. Something leapt to life in her green eyes, hints of her power shining through. My arousal throbbed again.

'You're welcome,' I said, the words gruffer than I'd intended them.

'I, erm,' she started, then bit her bottom lip. I almost groaned aloud as my attention was drawn to her mouth. 'I was talking to Hecate earlier and she said I should ask you about something.'

'OK.'

'It's sort of private.'

'Oh. Right.' I threw up the smoke bubble, and she looked around herself frowning.

'Won't this look really suspicious?' she asked me.

'No. To everyone else it looks like you're talking to an over-enthusiastic griffon.' A smile crossed her face.

'Let me see you?' I dropped the smoke that hid me from the world and saw her chest swell as she took a breath. 'How come you wear clothes from the mortal world instead of a toga?' she asked me.

'It pisses Zeus off,' I shrugged. 'Plus I look good in it.' I gave her my most wicked smile and she rolled her eyes at me.

'You think so, huh?'

'You'd prefer this?' I asked, and made my shirt vanish. Color leapt to her cheeks as her eyes widened. And I knew I wasn't imagining the lust I could see in them.

'Put your shirt back on!' she squeaked. My cock was throbbing painfully now, and I let my own desire show on my face as my shirt reformed around my chest.

'You said no magic sex!' she chided, and I bowed my head.

'So I did. I apologize profusely.'

'Liar.'

'What did you want to talk to me about?'

Her face changed, a seriousness settling over her beautiful features.

'Hecate said something about gods not being able to have more than one realm, and I should ask you about it because you can explain it better.'

'Hecate shouldn't be telling you anything about Olympus, because you're not staying here,' I snapped, the subject of her question causing the reality of the situation to slam back into me like a hammer.

Hurt flickered across her face, but she folded her arms and lifted her perfect chin.

'In that case, there's no harm in telling me,' she retorted.

The desire to talk to her like I used to, to have someone to share my problems with, made me want to tell her every secret I had, but I couldn't act on it. What good would it do? 'Tell me,' she demanded, and as I looked into her resolute face, my resolve crumpled a second time.

'Fine. Zeus is punishing me because I created a thirteenth realm and filled it with new life. I was able to keep it hidden from the other gods for a while, but eventually they found out. Zeus destroyed every living thing in it when he found it.' I was aware that my voice had gone hard with fury as I ground out the last sentence. Horror filled her eyes.

'Why?'

'As a punishment to me. But he fucked up. I was able to hide one of the creatures I had made. A sea creature who was turning out to be incredibly powerful. And once a realm has been created, it can not be destroyed, so I gave it to Oceanus before Zeus could work out what to do with it. Oceanus is one of the few beings he can't argue with.' I remembered the fury on my brother's face as he had agreed to the suggestion. He'd had no choice. And for a short time, I thought I'd won.

Until I'd seen *her*, standing in my throne room. 'Zeus announced the Hades Trials the next day, knowing how little I wanted to be married. His final act of revenge for my insolence was to find you and bring you back, knowing I'd either have to lose you again, or watch you die as a human.'

'What a complete fucking asshole,' she breathed, still wide-eyed.

'Yeah. Lord Asshole.'

'What happened to the sea creature you saved?'

'She's living under Oceanus's protection. It will be announced to the rest of Olympus that there is a new realm after these Trials are over. I think Zeus is still trying to find a way to stop it, but short of declaring war on Oceanus, I don't see how he can.'

Persephone stared up at me, her face intense and thoughtful.

'Why did you do it? Why risk his wrath like that?'

I pushed my hand through my hair, debating. Should I tell her the truth?

'After I lost you, I couldn't deal with the darkness,' I said quietly. 'You brought light and life to this place, and I became obsessed with replacing it.'

'So you made new life? Out of nothing?' She was staring at me now like I was crazy.

'Well, yeah. I didn't know if I could actually do it, and I had to have a lot of help from Hecate, but she's a Titan and much stronger than she lets on and-' I stopped talking as I realized I was babbling. Not a great trait in a king. I straightened, trying to reassert some dignity, but when I looked into Persephone's eyes they were filled with emotion.

'You literally created life to replace me?' she whispered.

'Yes. The hole you left in my heart was impossible to fill with anything less.'

'Did it work? Did it fill the hole?'

'No.'

. . .

She was in my arms in a heartbeat, her lips on mine with fervent desperation. Electricity sparked through my body, the mass of power I was permanently tempering deep inside me flaring to life. I pushed my hands into her hair, pulling her as close to me as was physically possible, every ounce of willpower deserting me completely as her desire swept through me.

'I need you,' she murmured onto my lips, lifting her hand to my jaw and pushing me back slightly, to look into my eyes. Hers were shining and intense, her pupils dilated. I moved one hand to the small of her back, pressing her against my hard body, and she tensed as she felt my arousal.

'I need you more,' I breathed, and a wicked gleam crossed her face.

'Is that right?' she whispered, and dropped her hand to her skirt. I was so hard I was beginning to worry that I wouldn't be able to contain myself.

Inch by tortuous inch, she began hitching up the long flowing material of her skirt. I took a deep breath as I watched more and more of her beautiful thighs being revealed, inhaling her divine scent. Just before she reached the top of the skirt she stopped, and moved her hand between her legs, out of view.

Oh gods, I was going to explode. I had to touch her. And this was the wrong place. She was too special, *this* was too special.

'You deserve to be worshiped,' I breathed. 'And I can't do that here. When I finally touch you I want to hear you scream my name, watch you come over and over.'

Her face flushed deeper red, her lips parting further. I ran my fingers along her jaw, drawing her face close to mine and kissed her again, deep and slow. She moaned softly as she kissed me back, and pleasure pounded through me. Or I could just take her here and now...

'You're right,' she said breathlessly, stepping back from me, her skirt dropping to the floor. 'We're supposed to be at a party.'

THIRTEEN

PERSEPHONE

I tried to concentrate on what people were saying to me, but it was almost impossible. I nodded absently as a wood-nymph told me for the fifth time that she thought it was super unfair that there had been a fake gem in my last trial. My mind was firmly stuck on Hades. He was like a freaking magnet to me, my rational thoughts turning to mush whenever I saw him. Although to be fair, I reckoned most girls would kiss a guy who created an entire world, life and all, to try to replace them. There was no question he had loved me. And there was zero doubt in my mind that any sexual chemistry we may have once had was still there.

'Persy!'

The voice was in my mind, and other than Hades' it was the one I had been most desperate to hear all evening.

'Skop!' I turned quickly, startling the girl who had been talking to me, and dropped to my knees as the little dog bounded towards me through the crowd. He skidded to a halt and wagged his tail furiously.

'Stop nearly dying! You're fucking killing me!'

I laughed loudly.

'I think you'll find I'm killing *me*,' I told him.

'They're total dicks for not giving you any tokens, you know. Total fucking dicks.'

'I agree. But at least I'm still alive.'

'You know, you really should eat another seed. Maybe with more power you'd be able to-'

'Slow down, hotstuff,' I said, standing again. 'My power was strong enough to break both my damn wrists. I don't need any more of that shit just now, thank you very much.'

'If you had more power, maybe you wouldn't have broken them. Or you'd be able to heal them faster if you had.'

'Let's not talk about this just now,' I said, noticing that the girl who had been talking to me was raising one eyebrow quizzically. 'Sorry,' I smiled at her. 'Just got to sort out my dog. It was nice to meet you.'

Skop followed me as I moved away from her, scanning the crowd for Hecate. I spotted her talking to Hedone and Morpheus. 'Where've you been anyway?' I asked Skop.

'Oh, erm, the water nymphs in the pool don't have any clothes on. I got a bit distracted.'

'Right. You were so glad to see me alive that you only ogled some naked women for half an hour before coming to talk to me.'

'Exactly. That's a pretty big deal. Half an hour of breasts is really not long enough to truly appreciate them.'

'Huh.'

'Especially when there are many breasts. In fact, now that I have ensured your safety I might just go back and check on them again.'

'Check on the many breasts?' I repeated.

'Yes.'

'See you later,' I sighed, and he trotted off towards the pool, tail wagging.

'That kobaloi is a menace,' I said as I reached my friends. Morpheus laughed and Hedone gave me a sympathetic look.

'They are known for being pests. I hope he's not giving you too much trouble?'

I immediately felt bad for moaning about Skop and shook my head quickly.

'No, no, he's fine really, as long as you're not a naked mermaid. I actually think he cares about me.'

'Really?' Morpheus raised his eyebrows in surprise.

'Yeah. As long as there are no breasts between him and me, I reckon he'd do whatever he could to keep me safe.'

'Well, he is your guard,' said Hecate. 'Did you chat to the boss?'

'Erm, yeah,' I answered, trying to keep any emotion from showing on my face.

'Oooo, always nice to spend time with the man you

might end up marrying,' beamed Hedone, and Morpheus wrapped his arm around her bare shoulders.

I stuck close to the three of them for the whole party, talking politely to anyone who came up to me, and doing my best to avoid Minthe and any of the gods. Hades flicked in and out of my view, always in smoke form, and always looking at me long enough to give me a glimpse of his silver eyes. I was already regretting doing the right thing and ending our brief encounter.

I listened to Hedone's husky voice as she pointed out various domes in the ocean, telling me about their famous inhabitants or shops. A huge group of turtles swam right up to us at one point, and I reached out delightedly as a little one turned somersaults. The dome was cool and solid, and could easily have been glass, though I suspected it was something more mysterious or godly than that. The little turtle bumped his head against the dome on the other side of my hand, then hurtled back towards his family, who were drifting away.

'This place is awesome,' I said. *And it could have belonged to Hades, if the brothers had been given different realms by Zeus...*

'Yes, it is one of my favorites,' Hedone replied.

'Where do you live?' I asked her.

'Pisces, Aphrodite's' realm.'

'What's it like?'

'A tropical paradise. It's very beautiful. And exclusive; not many are allowed to live there. But parties are frequent so many folk of importance have visited.'

'It sounds great,' I said. Hedone gave a soft laugh.

'I'm not sure it's the right place for someone who dislikes parties, or sharing their partners,' she said.

'Huh,' I answered. No. Maybe not my thing after all.

As amazing as Aquarius was, I found myself grateful when Hecate flashed us back to my rooms at the end of the evening. I was exhausted. And my head was still buzzing with what I had been told about Hades that night. One of the first things Hecate had said about him when I first got here was that he was different from the other gods, that he wasn't what he seemed. And she had been right.

'Skop, what does Dionysus think of Hades?' I asked the kobaloi as I climbed under the covers.

'*Bit of a weirdo. And grumpy.*'

'Hmmm.'

'*Why, you starting to like him?*'

'I might be, yeah.'

'*Well that can't be a bad thing, if you're going to marry him. Although why anyone would get married is beyond me.*'

'Limiting the number of breasts not appeal to you?' I asked him.

'*Nope. Definitely not. Unlimited breasts all the way, please.*'

I'd never thought about marriage much. I wasn't one

of those young girls who had a vision of their wedding day all planned out by the age of ten, but I also never gave it much consideration as a teenager, or even an adult. I'd never had a serious boyfriend before, because I simply never desired the company of any of the men I'd dated enough to keep seeing them. My brother said I was picky, and that I should keep it that way. He wanted the best for his little sister. I wondered what Sam would make of the King of the Underworld as my prospective partner, and the thought of his face if he ever saw Hades caused a bittersweet smile to settle on my lips.

Was the reason I'd never been interested in anyone before because I was meant to be with Hades? The passion I felt for him was so intense, I'd never felt anything like it before in my life. *Fated. Bonded.* If I went home, to New York, would I be destined to spend the rest of my life alone? Or with someone who would never make me feel... whatever it was Hades was doing to me?

Or was that just lust? If we gave in to our feelings, and got it all out of our systems, would the reality of the situation then just crash back in, leaving nothing but the death and darkness and secrets?

I let out a long breath. *Lose the Trials, stay alive, get back home.* That was plan and I had to stick to it.

Despite the fact that a mind-bendingly gorgeous god wanted to worship me.

Fire. There was fire. And pain. Someone had their hand

around my throat... I blinked and tried to thrash my head, and realized with a start that it was the man whose wife I had killed. His eyes were wild with madness, and my body was convulsing with pain. But I was lifting my hand, *Faesforos* ready to strike. I was going to kill him.

'No,' I tried to moan, but no sound came out of my mouth. I tried to stop my wrist. I deserved to die for what I'd done. Let him kill me. Let him take my life, in forfeit of his wife's. But the dagger kept moving, and my stomach twisted as I felt the tip pierce his flesh, then sink between his ribs.

I woke with a shout, gasping for breath and for a brief moment, I had no idea where I was.

'*Persy?*' Skop was on his feet in front of me and I stared at him, my pulse racing and sweat soaking my neck and back. '*Persy, what happened?*'

'A nightmare,' I breathed, bile in my throat. 'Just a nightmare.'

I'd been ready to kill that man. And not in the dream, in real life. In the ballroom that night. My body had responded without my head's intervention, my will to survive stronger than my revulsion at what needed to be done.

I was everything they said I was. There was a monster inside me, one that would kill to keep me alive.

I felt sick.

It was you or him. You did what anyone would have done, I tried to tell myself, my skin crawling.

.   .   .

I knew there was no way I could go back to sleep, my heart still hammering in my chest and the feel of the blade entering flesh so vivid in my mind. I stamped to my washroom and turned on the water on the shower, letting it run as hot as I could stand.

But it didn't help. Water couldn't wash away what I'd done to that man. I may not have actually ended his life, but I had been prepared to. And I had been the one who deserved to die if I really had killed his wife, not him.

The desire to hear that it wasn't my fault, to be absolved of my guilt, made me think of the Atlas garden. I needed to talk to the voice. *I needed to hear it wasn't my fault.*

'You OK?' asked Skop as I marched out of the washroom and back towards my bed.

'I'm going back to sleep,' I said firmly, pulling back the comforter and climbing into bed.

'Erm, yeah, good idea,' he said, jumping up with me. But rather than spin round in circles on the covers, then flopping onto his side as he usually did, he lay on his front, head resting on his paws alertly.

'I'm fine, Skop,' I told him. 'Just confused.'

It took what felt like hours to fall asleep again. My restless mind took me over and over things I couldn't make sense of, or didn't have enough information to understand.

But eventually, I heard birds chirruping, and the soft trickle of water, and the beautiful garden materialized around me. A wave of relief washed over me, cleansing the guilt and fear instantly. I walked towards the fountain, and saw that there were hundreds of butterflies on the rings making up Atlas's huge burden.

'They're stunning,' I murmured as I got close.

'*They are more than they appear to be,*' the voice answered.

'Yes. I imagine they are. Everything is.'

The voice chuckled.

'*You are learning, Persephone.*'

'I am angry,' I told him, sitting down on the fountain's edge.

'*Yes.*'

'I need to know if I should have died, instead of the man who attacked me.'

'*Little goddess, you are not to blame for the events in your life. Nor can you punish yourself for defending your own life. You are strong inside. Stronger than you allow yourself to be. And that is not wrong or bad.*'

'But I didn't know I could kill someone. I don't want to be able to kill someone.'

'*Olympus is not the same as the mortal world. You must not apply the same constraints.*'

'Surely death is death, wherever you are.'

There was a long pause, and I swirled my fingers through the water. The butterflies leapt into the air as one, and I stared up at the mass of colors as they beat their tiny wings.

'*The only way to find out about your past and recon-cile yourself with your future is to get your memories back.*'

'How? Hades won't tell me.'

'*The river Lethe.*'

'Where is it?'

'*I do not know, but if you have your powers, you will be able to find it. Why have you not eaten another seed yet?*'

'The vines frightened me,' I admitted, looking out across the garden. The sunflowers were swaying slightly in the breeze.

'*You will be less frightened the next time. And those around you will teach you how to use them safely.*'

'You told me not to trust the people around me.'

'*And you mustn't. But you can learn from them.*'

I nodded.

'OK.'

'*Thank you for visiting me, little goddess,*' he said, and the garden vanished.

FOURTEEN

PERSEPHONE

'I honestly don't know why it's taken you this long,' said Hecate, staring at the pomegranate seed in my hand. When she had knocked on my door the following morning, I had asked her to stay with me while I ate the next seed. Just in case.

'I told you, I didn't want to overwhelm myself,' I told her.

She rolled her eyes at me.

'Fine, whatever. Just eat the seed.'

'And you'll stop my power doing anything crazy? If I lose control?' I asked her, peering seriously into her face.

'Yes, yes, I already told you, I will make sure you don't do anything crazy.'

'Good.'

I took a deep breath, and looked at the little seed. The vines had helped me on Aquarius, without them I probably would have died. And the feeling when they had turned green in the conservatory... If I could be taught how to use my powers properly, and safely, then they might be what I needed to survive the next five Trials. *And find the river Lethe and get my memories back.*

Before I could talk myself out of it, I popped the seed into my mouth. Last time, I'd been too out of it, too desperate and in pain to notice the taste, but this time... It was sharp and sweet and completely delicious.

'Mmmm,' I mumbled.

'Feel any different? Like you wanna blow some shit up?' Hecate's eyes were alive with excitement.

I swallowed.

'No.'

Apart from a very slight tingle, I felt nothing. Hecate's face fell.

'Oh. How disappointing.'

'I worry about you,' I told her.

'Probably wise.'

I sighed and looked around my bedroom, restless and nervous. I hadn't really expected a burst of power on eating the second seed, but I now felt relieved and frustrated in equal parts.

'I'm sick of this room, can we go somewhere else? How about a tour of the Underworld?'

'No-can-do, I'm afraid.'

'Why not? If I'm competing to live here, I should probably know more about it.'

'I agree, but you're not allowed out until Round Three.'

I scowled.

'Of course I'm not. In that case I'm going to the conservatory.'

'OK. But don't forget the next Trial is being announced this evening.'

'How the hell am I going to forget that?' I said, opening my bedroom door and frowning at her, but she was looking down at my feet. I followed her gaze.

Ice cold dread slid down my spine as I stared at a child's doll on the floor, just outside my door. It was charred and burned, and a note was pinned to its front, the word written on it clear as day. *'Murderer.'*

Hecate was next to me in a flash, her eyes turning white as she looked at the doll. I felt my heart begin to pound, fear and revulsion crawling up my throat.

'It's not magic, or dangerous,' she said as Skop appeared on my other side.

'It's... It's a message,' I whispered.

'It's fucked up,' said Skop, his usually playful voice hard.

'Did I kill a child?' I looked up at Hecate, unable to keep the hot tears from burning the back of my eyes. 'Please, please tell me I didn't kill a child.'

The thought was utterly unbearable, my head spinning as I formed the plea.

'Of course you didn't. Someone is trying to scare you, that's all,' Hecate answered, her face more angry than I'd ever seen it.

'Who?'

'I don't know. But Hades needs to know about this.

Stay in your room,' she said, and reached down for the doll. Images flashed into my mind as I stared at it. Images from dreams I'd had all my life. Bodies burning around me, men, women and children alike. 'Skop, guard this door,' Hecate said, then slammed the door shut and vanished, taking the awful burned doll with her.

'What if I deserve this? What if I am a murderer?'

'Persy, I haven't known you very long, but I seriously doubt that,' said Skop.

'You don't remember me from before though. When I was married to a god who rips people apart, and spent time with twisted lunatics who torture and play with folk for fun. They tried to drown you in fucking sand, for entertainment! And I used to be one of them!'

Tears were streaming down my face as my voice rose, and Skop finally looked from the closed door to me.

'Olympus is dangerous. Anyone born here accepts that. If you play with fire, you'll get burned. I knew the risk I was taking when I accepted the job of guarding you. And you need to accept that who you used to be isn't who you are now. Move on.'

'How can I move on when it's on my fucking doorstep?' A black vine burst from my palm, smashing into the aforementioned door with the power of a freight train. The wood splintered as I screamed, and Skop bounded out of the way as the vine whipped back towards us.

A wall of black smoke shot up in front of me, the vine slowing abruptly, like it was moving through treacle.

'Send the vine away, Persephone,' rang out Hades'

voice. The anger and fear inside me had built up too much momentum now though, and I was no longer thinking clearly.

'Don't tell me what to do!' I roared, and pulled on the vine. The smoke held it, and a bolt of rage made me yank harder. 'Stop fucking toying with me! All of you!'

Hades stepped through the smoke, and locked his eyes on mine. The rage inside me stuttered and he closed his hand slowly around my trapped vine. Black lines instantly began to spread from the vine across his skin, snaking around his fingers, then the rest of his hand. I watched, open-mouthed, as they flowered in front of me, tiny black leaves forming like tattoos, now disappearing under the cuff of his shirt.

A new energy began to hum through me, dark and strong and deliciously powerful.

'What are you doing?' I whispered, the feeling exquisite, but some part of me knowing it was wrong.

'I'm doing nothing. You are doing this.' With his other hand he reached up and deftly unbuttoned his shirt. It fell open, revealing the black vines now spreading across his chest, coiling around his hard muscles. 'When they reach my heart, they'll try to take my power.'

I recoiled at his words, and the vine vanished from my palm instantly. The blissful, powerful feeling ebbed away fast, the tattoo snaking across Hades' body fading to nothing just as quickly.

'Take your power?' My breathing was shallow, and I was already dizzy.

'Yes. You would never be able to; I am too strong and my power is too well guarded.'

'Is that what that feeling was? Your power?'

'My defensive power, yes. You've exerted yourself again, you need to sit.'

I wanted to argue, but my legs felt weak. I'd passed out from using my powers twice before, and I wasn't stupid enough to deny his words. I stumbled backwards until I felt my bed behind me, and sat. Hades flicked his hand without his gaze leaving my face, and a new door appeared behind him, in place of the shattered one.

'Why did my vine try to steal your power?'

'All gods have weapons, Persephone. That is yours.' He approached me slowly, then waved his wrist again, a goblet appearing in his hand. He offered it to me and I took it with shaking hands. Without even looking inside it, I gulped it down, the sluggishness slowly receding as I tasted wine.

Hades sat down on the bed beside me. 'We all have different types of power. Your black vines are aggressive. But you have other powers too. Like the green vines, that give life to things that grow.'

I stared at him, tangled emotions still bubbling inside me.

'The blue light around you when you killed that man. The one that turned into corpses...' He nodded.

'That is my aggressive power. I draw it from the dead.'

I shuddered. It sounded like something from a horror film.

'Who left that doll on my doorstep?'

'I don't know yet. But I will find out.' His jaw was tense and his eyes glittered with ferocity.

'Is the note on it true? Was I a murderer?'

'No, Persephone.'

'But I stabbed that man.'

'He was choking the life from you. Anyone in this world would have reacted as you did, and anyone in your world too.'

'Not if they deserved to die.'

Heat seared around me, Hades' eyes turning from silver to electric blue.

'Don't you dare say that, Persephone. That piece of shit who tried to kill you, and his friends, are enemies of mine, not yours. Once again, you are being targeted as a result of my misdeeds. I am sorry.'

Hope blossomed through me at his words. Could that be true? I drained the rest of the wine, trying to order my chaotic thoughts and slow my racing pulse. Hades would find whoever had left the doll. And the voice in the garden had given me a somewhat vague plan, but a plan nonetheless, to get my memories back. Right now, my most pressing issue was these damned vines.

'You said you would teach me to use my magic,' I said, handing him back the goblet. His eyes melted back to silver, the temperature dropping again.

'Yes. And I will teach you to fight. Starting now.'

'Now?'

'Yes.'

FIFTEEN

PERSEPHONE

'So how is it you keep showing up when I need you?'
I asked as I walked alongside Hades through the
blue torchlit corridors. I had insisted we walk to the
training room. The less flashing about, the better, in my
opinion. I felt small as we walked, his broad shoulders
filling the space and his height so much greater than
mine. But I felt safe, rather than intimidated.

'I told you, your power is like a beacon to me.'

'What does it look like?' He looked sideways at me.

'Green light.'

'You and Hecate both glow blue,' I said.

'Yes. Most of the time. That's the color I chose for
Underworld power.'

'Who chose green for me then?'

'Your mother. She chose green for all nature powers.'

My steps faltered. *My mother*.

'But I already have parents. At home.' My words were
slow and Hades stopped walking, turning to me.

'I know. But before that... You had a mother here. The goddess of the harvest,' he said gently.

'Demeter?' I asked slowly, remembering my classics lessons.

'Yes.'

'Where- where is she now?'

'She hasn't been seen in Olympus since not long after you were born.'

'Oh. Who was my father?'

'Nobody knows.'

So to add to the long list of things my head wouldn't properly process, I now had the fact that my parents weren't really my parents.

I expected to feel sadness, or anger, but instead all I felt was a kind of hollow indifference. I mean, on some level I must have realized I had a family in Olympus when I accepted that this place was real, I just never properly put the two together or let myself consider it. What did it matter? As far as I was concerned, my real family were in New York, safe and sound, and there was no way I would ever entertain the idea of anyone else being my parents or brother. Maybe I was birthed elsewhere, but that was just biology.

'Who brought me up, if my mom and dad were missing?' I asked Hades.

'Wood and forest nymphs. On Taurus.'

'Taurus? Who owns Taurus?'

'*Dionysus*,' Skop answered in my head at the same time Hades said the wine god's name. I looked down at the little dog.

'So that's why you're here? That's why Dionysus volunteered a guard?' He wagged his tail.

'It took years for you to tell me that, by the way,' Hades said, resuming walking. 'I don't think you ever told anyone else. You just arrived at one of Aphrodite's parties one day, looking outrageously gorgeous, and announced yourself as Demeter's daughter, goddess of Spring.'

'Seriously?' I hurried to catch up with him, tearing my eyes from where they'd involuntarily glued themselves to his ass.

'Yup. I knew there and then that you were no normal goddess.'

'How long were we married for?'

He paused before answering.

'Four years.'

'That's not long for an immortal god,' I said slowly.

'No. It is not.'

Sadness rolled from him, and I felt a pull in my gut as though I were physically wired into his emotions. I tried to think of something helpful to say, but nothing came.

We walked in silence the rest of the way to the training room, Hades opening the door for me when we got there.

'Now, you realize that I will have to make you angry in order for us to do this?'

'Angry is fine. But try not to scare the shit out of me again,' I said, walking onto the training mats.

'I won't,' he said quietly. 'As I told you, we all have our powers. One of mine is to make people feel their worst fears. In fact, I have a dog who has the same power.'

'You have a dog?' I turned and gaped at him.

'Yes. Several, actually. But Cerberus is the most important.'

'Wait, doesn't he have three heads?'

Hades nodded.

'Yes. I assume he exists in your human mythology?'

'Yeah, and he's sort of terrifying.'

'He's about as terrifying as I am,' Hades chuckled, rolling up his sleeves. I cocked my head at him.

'You realize that's pretty terrifying, right?'

His beautiful face turned serious as the smile slipped away.

'Yes. I do. But not all of my powers revolve around fear.' He held his hand up, palm facing me. 'Give me your dagger.'

I pulled *Faesforos* from the sheath around my thigh and hesitated, before handing it to him. In a flash he had taken the knife and drawn it across his raised palm. I gasped as gold blood ran from the wound, trickling down his forearm.

'What are you-'

'Gods' blood is called ichor. And it is gold. But that's not what I want to show you.' The cut began to glow silver, the same color as his eyes, and then the skin was knitting back together, sealing the wound. 'Healing is something you must learn as these Trials get more dangerous. Your body will do some of the work while you rest, but you must learn more immediate healing.'

'What other types of magic are there?'

'Many, many types. You already know, and dislike,

the power that transports us places. Only very powerful gods can do that. Lust and love are commonly held gifts though. As is the power to make others angry.'

'What powers do I have?'

'Your black vines defend you both by their physical use and their ability to drain other's power. Your green vines make things grow, adding strength to nature. Your...' He trailed off, his eyes locking onto mine. 'It's probably not worth going into that until we know if you have regained that particular power.'

I felt my face crease into a frown.

'What? What particular power?'

Hades whole body had stiffened.

'We'll go into that if it comes up,' he repeated, his voice stern. Indignation rose like a tidal wave through me.

'I'm not a child,' I snapped. That dangerous spark flared in his eyes.

'I am your King,' he replied, voice cold and hard. 'You will do as you are bid.' Black smoke began to flicker around him.

I didn't know if he was deliberately goading me to get me to use my power, or being an actual prick, but either way, it was the only trigger I needed.

'Will I fuck,' I answered, and lifted my palms, willing the black vines into existence. They burst from my hands and I felt a surge of delight as they went exactly where I wanted them to.

Hades stood his ground as they hit him, instantly beginning to coil around his shoulders. He narrowed his eyes at me, a small smile spreading across his lips as he spoke.

'I like this shirt, and I have a feeling you're going to try to make a mess of it.' With a little blue shimmer his shirt vanished, and I felt my vines go slack as my concentration vanished, the sight of his bare skin taking all of my focus.

Then a wave of power hit me and I stumbled backwards. I jerked my wrists, making the vines taut again and pulling on them to stop myself falling.

'Bastard,' I growled. 'That's not fair.'

His eyes were dark with something that could definitely have been lust, and a tight black t-shirt suddenly covered his perfect body and I squashed the stab of disappointment.

'Better?' he said, and another wave of power slammed into me. I gripped my vines harder, trying to work out what I could do next.

'Much,' I lied, and tried to remember what it had felt like when the vines had turned into the tattoos.

But I'd been furious and scared then. I still had plenty of pent up frustration and tension roiling through me, but when I was with Hades like this, I couldn't access that primal rage, that fear that drove me to lose control. The only thing I was going to lose control of here was my grip on my desire for him. Especially if he lost his shirt again.

A little bolt of anticipation charged through me as I glared at his impossibly beautiful face, remembering his words. 'I want to worship you.' I saw his eyes flick to the vines wrapped around his chest, then widen as he looked back at me. His expression changed completely, a predatory hunger filling his face. His lips parted, and he reached up with both hands and pulled on the vines. I stumbled towards him with a yelp, then my breath caught.

My vines were gold. Shining, glittering gold.

'I guess it's time we talked about your other power after all,' Hades said, his voice deep and low and so loaded with desire it made my core clench. 'Your gold vines do the opposite of the black ones. They share your power.' He was breathing hard, and slowly reeling me towards him.

'What do you mean?' I asked, making a show of trying to pull against him, but it was a half-assed attempt. The truth was, I wanted nothing more than to be pulled into him completely.

'When your gold vines do this,' he said turning his forearms towards me so that I could see the gold vine tattoos swirling around them, 'I can feel what you're feeling.'

I stopped tugging, and my mouth fell open. Heat leapt to my face.

'You can feel what I'm feeling? Like mind-reading?'

'Let me show you,' he said, barely audibly.

Blue light began to shine along the gold vines, starting at his body, then whizzing along them, back towards me. When they reached my palms, I gasped.

I could *feel* his desire for me. More, I could see it. Images flashed through my mind of the two of us in the largest bed I'd ever seen, but I barely noticed the beautiful posts and black drapes adorning it because oh my gods, I was seeing and feeling it through his eyes. He was staring down at me laying on the sheets before him, naked and holy fuck, I looked a million times better than I really did. A series of images began to flash before me, so fast I couldn't hold onto a single one; me sinking onto his lap, him burying his face between my thighs, me bending over before him and spreading myself, his length hard and pounding and ready.

'Oh gods,' I moaned aloud, and the images stopped abruptly. I opened my eyes and saw my own lust mirrored in Hades' wild eyes. 'You said no magic sex!' I panted.

'You started it!'

'What?'

'That's what these do,' he said through gritted teeth as he lifted my gold vines. 'You're sending me images like that right now.'

'What!' I yelped, and the gold vines vanished instantly. Hades sagged slightly, before standing straight again, eyes still wild. 'Why didn't you tell me I had magic sex powers!' I demanded, trying and failing to ignore the urgent need between my legs.

'Because I didn't know if they were back or not.' My eyes flicked to his groin. I'd just got a glimpse of what was in his jeans, and now I couldn't shift it. I didn't just want him. *I needed him.* The pounding was becoming painful, and I squirmed where I stood. Either we were going to fuck right now, or I needed to be wherever he wasn't.

'Maybe we should try the training later,' he ground

out. Guttural disappointment hit me in the gut. *But I need you.* 'Hecate can teach you healing before the next Trial.'

'Right,' I said tightly. He looked into my face.

'I'm sorry, Persephone. If I stay here a second longer, I won't be able to stop myself.'

Then he vanished before I could tell him he didn't have to.

SIXTEEN

HADES

For the love of all the fucking gods, the gold vines were back. That was me done for. There was no fucking way I could resist her, glowing green and gold and showing me every delicious thing she wanted me to do to her. I turned the temperature in the shower down even further, blasting my body with freezing water. It wouldn't work, but short of fucking Persephone senseless I didn't know what else to try. There was no way I was going to relieve myself with someone else, and doing it myself had stopped working centuries before.

It was getting harder and harder to believe that I was going to be able to let her go. If she regained all of her power, if those gold vines ended up able to share more than just her sexual desires...

Memories of her wrapped around me, of our bodies entwined, those beautiful vines filling my monstrous heart with life and light. I'd told her that she had changed the Underworld when she had been here, made it brighter. I had told her that I had tried to create life to replace the hole her absence had left inside me. But she couldn't know that she was the only chance I had at reversing the damage this place had done to me. The damage my brother had done to me.

I hadn't started out as a monster. I had found taking life more repulsive than most of my siblings, in fact. Which was why Zeus thought me weak, and favored Poseidon. For the first few decades of my new role, dealing with the dead had saddened me. I felt pity and empathy for the souls arriving in my realm. But that was unsustainable. As King it was my job to judge the guilty. I wasn't expected to bother with petty thieves or remorseful adulterers, but I had to deal with the scum of Olympus, the worst of every species alive. Day after day I saw and heard of the increasing levels of brutality mortals were capable of, their motives always shallow and selfish. The more punishments I had to dole out for their unspeakable acts, the less I cared for them.

And as my brothers' realms flourished, and they both found wives, my sadness turned to bitterness.

Those punishments started to become a way to vent my building anger. I started out telling myself that those receiving them deserved them, ignoring the fact that I was now enjoying watching men flayed alive, or flesh burning from skin. Ignoring the fact that the well of power that had always burned hot inside me was darkening, twisting, dirtying.

The more horrific my punishments of the guilty became, the more my brothers seemed to respect me. Before long, they left me alone, content that I was doing the job that Zeus had bestowed on me. I surrounded myself in smoke, banned everyone from my realm, and let myself become the monster the King of the Underworld needed to be.

But then I met Persephone. Somehow, she alone recognized what was buried deep inside me. And the same life-giving power she used to nurture and grow plants had flowed into me through those gleaming vines for four years, healing parts of me I thought lost forever.

Until she was ripped away.

Before I knew what I was doing I had slammed my fist into the marble wall of the shower. It cracked, collapsing completely, water spraying across the room.

'For fuck's sake!' I shouted, and stamped my foot. It instantly repaired itself. *What was I going to do?* I wasn't sure I could cope with losing her again.

The rest of the day dragged painfully slowly, my mind slipping back to the images Persephone had sent me almost constantly.

'Boss, pay attention, this is important,' said Hecate, snapping me out of an intense vision of Persephone's soft lips wrapped around the tip of my cock.

'Sorry, what?' I asked, shifting uncomfortably in my seat. Stupid fucking erection.

'Kerato says he has news. On the Spring Undead faction.' I sat up, immediately alert.

'I'll see him in the throne room now.'

'My Lord,' the minotaur bowed low as I flashed onto my throne.

'What news do you have?'

'We have captured someone known to be closely associated with the attacker.'

'Where is he now?'

'*She* is in the holding pits.'

'Bring her to me.'

Rage simmered inside me, the memory of what that man had almost done to my Queen making my blood boil in my veins. And under the rage danced the twisted excitement that accompanied the knowledge that I was about to inflict primal terror on a living being. That I was going to become their worst nightmare, their whole world, that I held their pitiful life in my hands.

I glanced at the rose throne. When Persephone had been seated beside me, I had been able to control the excitement. Subdue it, even. But in the time she had been gone the excitement had returned, the monster inside me able to rear its ugly head again, to feed off fear and death.

A greedy thrill went through me like a tremor, the dark well of power rippling in anticipation as Kerato marched back in five minutes later, a bedraggled woman following him in chains.

'What is your name?' I asked her, making my voice sound like a thousand slithering serpents and the smoke surrounding me icy cold.

'Daphne,' she answered, as she sank to her knees in front of me. Her voice was too strong, too defiant. Dark tension gripped my body.

'And you knew Calix?'

'He was my brother.' She kept her gaze on the floor, hunched low over her knees. Dirty blonde hair obscured her face from my view completely.

I hated her.

'Your brother tried to kill Persephone.'

'Yes.'

'Why?'

'She killed his wife.'

'How do you know that?' This was what I needed to find out, before I ended her miserable life. This was what made no sense to me, what posed a real danger. Nobody should remember Persephone, outside my closest advisors and the other eleven Olympians.

'I-I just do,' she said.

I sent out a tendril of smoke towards her and my magic dove inside her mind, gleefully tearing through it to find what was buried deepest, what scared her more than anything else in the world.

She shrieked, tipping her head back, eyes wide with fear.

'Stop! Please!'

'Tell me how you know about Persephone.'

'When we saw her in the Hades Trials we just suddenly knew,' she gasped, tears streaming down her face. 'Please, please make it stop.'

'How did you know?'

'We saw it. Calix and I saw what happened and he remembered his wife.' Her skin had gone as pale as snow but I was too focused on my questions to care what she was seeing.

'What about the rest of the so-called Spring Undead?'

'They all saw too, as soon as she appeared in the flame dishes. They all remembered who they had lost.' I was struggling to understand her words through her sobs, and I retracted my smoke just a little. She fell forward immediately.

'How many are there?'

'I've only met two others,' she choked.

'Name them.'

'Nicos and Lander.' I looked at Kerato.

'Lander was the first man we captured, he is dead,' the minotaur said gruffly. The woman wailed. 'We shall search for this Nicos now.'

'Good. Take her back to the pits, and keep her alive. We may be able to use her.' If there were more of these fools then she might come in useful as bait.

I barely heard the woman's sobs as Kerato hauled her out of the throne room. How had these people remembered what had happened? It was impossible without the water from the river Lethe. And the location of the river was one of closest guarded secrets in Virgo. The thought of someone within my own realm conspiring against me made my body burn with anger, the unspent tension inside me crackling to life. The colored flames around the edges of the room leapt up, all flashing brightest blue in unison. I would crush every last member of this Spring Undead, and I would make sure whoever was behind it spent an eternity in the living hell that was Tartarus.

SEVENTEEN

PERSEPHONE

It was a good thing, really, that Hades had left before anything had happened, I thought, sending a little green vine from my palm into the soil of the flower bed. A delicious energy hummed through me, making my skin tingle. An image of Hades, eyes dark and deep with lust as he looked up at me from between my legs, flashed into my mind. I felt a surge of power from the vine and gaped as a shoot leaped up in front of me. I pulled the vine back and the pale green shoot slowed to a stop.

'I'm gonna guess that was a result of you thinking about loverboy,' said Skop. I turned to him, too surprised to argue. He shook his little dog head, and resumed digging in the dirt. For a dog that wasn't really a dog, he sure loved to dig.

'Knock knock,' sang Hecate's voice from the doorway of the conservatory. I stood up quickly.

'Hi,' I called, and turned to see her sauntering between the flowerbeds towards me.

. . .

'It doesn't look much more green in here yet,' she said as she looked about herself.

'Well, I think I just found out how to make things grow quicker,' I said, gesturing to the shoot.

'Ooh, what is it?'

'A sweet pea.'

'Nice. The Trial announcement is going to be made over the flame dishes tonight, so no showy ceremonies or dicking around.' I tried to stop my face from falling, but must have failed because Hecate frowned at me. 'I thought you'd be pleased? You always say you hate all that shit.'

But now I wouldn't be able to see him again tonight.

'Oh, yeah, I just...' I scrabbled for something to say, but Hecate looked sharply at Skop, then back at me, a slow smile spreading across her face.

'You were hoping to see Hades tonight,' she said, glee in her voice.

'Skop! You snitch!'

'*I told her nothing,*' he said, without looking at me.

'Bullshit.'

'*Well, she's practically his best friend. She'll know soon anyway that you two are hooking up.*'

'We're not hooking up!'

'*Then why does he hide you or me in smoke literally every time he's with you?*'

'Privacy from perverted gnomes,' I said, my face burning.

'Cos you're banging.'

'We are not banging!' My protest was so enthusiastic that I said the words out loud by accident and Hecate gave a bark of laughter.

'You and I, dear Persy, need to have a catch up. With wine. How about we watch the trial announcement at my place tonight, and have a few drinks? A girls' night.'

'That sounds awesome,' I said, surprised by how much I meant it. That really did sound like exactly what I needed. An evening with Hecate, and no Hades anywhere. A chance to clear my head.

Hecate's rooms were significantly nicer than mine, though not my taste. She had to flash me there, because I wasn't allowed anywhere other than the conservatory and the training room, and we arrived in a large sitting room. Rocky walls and the high ceiling glowing with dusky daylight provided illumination, but the room had a dark, elegant feel to it. The floor was covered in deep plush carpet in a dark grey and two black gothic style couches with ornate detailing over the curved wooden frames dominated the room. The wall on my right was made up of a giant black bookcase, full to the brim with leather-bound volumes. The opposite wall had a long counter running along it, made of a dark wood and similarly gothic in style, and abstract geometric art in hundreds of shades of blue hung on the wall above it. The counter was covered in exotic looking objects, and I was half way to picking up a glowing skull before Hecate stopped me.

'Do not touch that,' she said sharply, and I froze.

'OK. Why not?'

'You'll wake up Kako. And I am not dealing with his shit tonight.'

'Kako?'

'The evil spirit that lives in that skull.'

'Riiiight,' I said, staring at the skull. 'Of course there's an evil spirit living in your sitting room.'

'Well, I am the goddess of ghosts,' she shrugged, and bent to open one of the many cupboards under the counter.

'Is there anything else I shouldn't touch?' I asked, looking along the row of shiny, glowing items. There was a vial that had something neon orange in it, a curved blade with tiny swirls etched all over it, a large pearl that shimmered in the low light coming from the wall behind it, and many other things besides. I wanted to touch it all.

'Everything. Leave it all alone.'

I pulled a face but backed away from the counter. The back wall of the room was missing, a large archway in its place, and I could see a massive four poster bed draped with black sheer material in the room beyond. A memory of the bed I'd seen Hades and I in popped into my head and I turned away quickly, sitting down on one of the couches.

'So, where's your flame dish?' I asked.

'Oh, yeah,' she said, straightening and setting two glasses on the counter. Her eyes turned white as she glowed blue, then a massive iron dish on a short stand appeared in front of the couch. A gentle orange flame flickered to life in the center. I peered at it.

'So these are like TVs? Do they always have something showing?'

'You can use them to talk to each other, like your video phones, or the gods can broadcast on them. That's it.'

'And people in Olympus have been watching me in the Trials so far in these?'

'Yup.'

'Mental,' I breathed.

'So are your video phones. Athena is so proud of your current civilization. You've got pretty far pretty quickly.'

'Huh,' I said. I couldn't think about my world as an experiment of a bored god. It made my head hurt too much, so I changed the subject.

'What are we drinking?'

'My specialty cocktail,' she said. 'But I'm missing something. Wait here. And don't touch anything!'

Hecate flashed out of the room and Skop immediately jumped onto the couch with me.

'Touch the skull! Please, please touch the skull!' His tail was wagging at a million miles an hour as he looked pleadingly at me.

'No! Not a chance,' I told him, avoiding looking at it. I wanted to touch it very much.

'You're so boring,' he humpfed, and sat down.

'You know, Skop, of the many words I could use to describe myself right now, boring isn't one of them. I have magic sex power for fuck's sake.'

'*What?*'

'Yeah.'

'*I want magic sex power,*' he said.

'I thought you were already a god in bed.'

His tail wagged.

'*I sure am.*'

Hecate flashed back into the room holding a large metal jug before he could elaborate, thankfully.

'How come you couldn't just conjure whatever that is?'

'I can conjure wine, not this,' she said, a wicked edge to her voice. I raised my eyebrows as she poured something lime green from the jug into two glasses. I swear there was smoke coming from it.

'Are you sure you've made this before?' I asked tentatively.

'Yup. And now you have your power back, you can drink it.' She added more things, with her back to me so I couldn't see, then strode over to the couch and handed me the cocktail. It was still green, but it smelled like cherries.

'What's it called?'

'Spartan spirit.'

'Well, cheers,' I said, clinking my glass against hers then taking a sip. There was an explosion of fruit in my mouth, bitter cherry and sour blackberry and sweet strawberries all at once, tingling across my tongue. 'This is amazing!'

'I know,' she said, taking a long sip of her own as she sat beside me. 'Oooh, look!' I raised my eyes from my new favorite drink, to see the flames in the fire dish leaping high and burning white hot. They faded as a crystal clear image of the commentator appeared in the center of the dish.

'Good evening Olympus!'

'Urgh, I hate him,' I muttered.

'Yeah, he's fucking irritating,' agreed Hecate.

'I'm sure you're all dying to know what our little Persephone is going to be facing next!' *Our little Persephone?* Gods, I wanted to smack him in the face. 'She has mostly faced tests of glory or hospitality so far.' Apprehension skittered through my belly. The other two values were intelligence and loyalty. 'Well, the wait is over! Tomorrow afternoon she will be facing her first intelligence Trial!'

'Does that mean no nearly dying?' I asked, turning to Hecate. She screwed her face up apologetically.

'Probably not, no.'

'Here is your host to tell you more,' the commentator said, and faded from view. My breath caught as the black smoke of Hades shimmered into existence, his throne room visible behind him. It was strange now to see him made of smoke, translucent and rippling, when I knew what perfection lay underneath.

'As Queen of the Underworld, Persephone would be expected to abide in my realm,' he said and his voice was tight and cold. A shiver rippled over me. 'We must therefore test her ability to survive in dangerous environments.

She will be trapped in a deadly part of Virgo and must escape.' He made a small hissing sound, then vanished.

I looked at Hecate, nerves crackling.

'Where will they trap me?'

'I don't know, but he sounded seriously pissed. There is no way this was his idea.' Hecate looked worried. 'This is Zeus' doing, he's forcing Hades to expose more of his realm to the world. Gods that guy is a dick.'

I took a long swig of my drink and nodded.

'Yeah. He really is.'

Neither of us spoke for a long few minutes, then I cleared my throat.

'I probably shouldn't drink too much, if I have to compete tomorrow.'

Hecate snorted.

'You have healing power now, you won't get a hangover.'

'Are you serious?'

'Yeah.'

'No more hangovers? Ever?'

'Uhuh.'

'How the hell is everyone here not permanently drunk?'

'Some are, to be fair. Me included.' I laughed and had another big gulp of my spartan spirit, just because I could. 'If they're going to trap you somewhere, we should probably try to work out what you might need to take with you. Are you claustrophobic?'

'No more than the next person,' I said, thinking. 'Like if you trap me in a burning room, I'll panic.' I smiled, but

Hecate didn't. 'Oh. Are they going to trap me in a burning room?'

'I'm not going to lie to you, Persy, quite a lot of the Underworld is made up of burning rooms.'

'Shit.'

'Yeah. Take *Faesforos*, and use your vines. If it's an intelligence test then you'll need to solve some sort of puzzle or answer a riddle to get out.'

I groaned.

'If it's like the ball and it's all gods and stuff, I won't be able to do it.'

'Honestly, it could be anything.'

'Should we go over some basic god stuff now, just in case?' I asked her.

She raised one eyebrow at me doubtfully.

'Persy, do you have any idea how long it takes to learn the history of the gods? There are literally whole schools here to teach that.'

'Oh.' I thought about that. Schools in Olympus must be pretty different to the hell-hole I'd attended. 'What was your school like?' I asked her.

'I didn't go to school. I'm a Titan.'

I frowned.

'So?'

'So, up until recently, Zeus wouldn't let Titans be trained in the academies. Athena has since convinced him that us dangerous Titan offspring are safer under their supervision, but he still hates us. As do a lot of Olympus.'

'Why? I mean, I know about the war and stuff, but

that was forever ago wasn't it?'

'Titans are strong. They are the original gods. So when they turn nasty, they're like, seriously nasty. And that scares people.'

'Aren't all the really bad ones in Tartarus though?'

'Yeah, and there hasn't been a genocidal Titan in thousands of years, but it doesn't stop stories being told to fuel the fear.' Her eyes were tight and frustrated, and I thought about what Hades had said. *Hecate is much stronger than she lets on.*

'Do you hide your power so that people don't fear you?' I asked hesitantly. Her eyes locked on mine, and it took her a while to answer.

'I used to, yes. But over the time I've lived here with Hades I've come to trust him. And I've built up a reputation in Virgo. People don't fuck with me anymore.'

Any more? Was Hecate bullied too? The way Eris had spoken to her at the ball, mocking her Titan heritage, flashed into my memory. How in the hell could Hades and Hecate, two of the most badass people I'd *ever* met have been victims of bullying? Determination filled me, sending strength and courage coursing through my veins. If they had overcome their past and their enemies, and become as powerful as they had, then so could I. And I bet they had both put up with worse than Ted Hammond's groping hands and taunting jibes. *Have they not gone too far though?* The doubt constantly present inside me forced the question to the surface, but I shoved it back down again.

'I'm starving. What are we eating?'

EIGHTEEN

PERSEPHONE

'So, is Skop right, are you sleeping with Hades?'

Hecate asked the question so casually I almost choked on my beef.

'No! Skop is not right!'

'You want to though,' she ginned.

'Hecate, what happens when Olympians get married? Hades said something about a bond, but he was infuriatingly vague.'

'I dunno,' she shrugged. 'I'm not an Olympian. They marry for life though. No divorces at the top.'

'*Told ya,*' said Skop, gnawing on a steak at my feet.

'You know, you two were a great couple.'

'He's kinda... intense,' I said carefully.

'No shit. You should have seen him when you left.'

A bolt of pain gripped my chest at the thought, and I was surprised by its strength.

'He said you helped him. With the thirteenth realm.'

Hecate's face changed slightly, a less sassy smile

replacing her usual expression, something deeper peeking through.

'He told you about that?'

'Yes.'

'Good. I want you to win this, Persy. I don't know what happened before, or why you left, but I swear whatever it was can't be as bad as you leaving again. I've known Hades a long time. Like, a really long time. The few years you were together, he almost became his true self again.'

Her words seemed to physically pound into me, as though hearing them from someone other than him made them even more real, more undeniable. How was it possible that I could have had this much of an impact on someone's life, and up until now I hadn't even known they existed? And not just anyone, *a freaking god*.

'I'm drawn to him in a way I've never felt before,' I admitted. 'I can't explain it.' Hecate stood up, gathering our empty glasses.

'Well he is sexy as fuck,' she said, as she strode to the counter.

'I think it might be more than that. I'm worried... I'm worried that now I've met him, nobody will ever make me feel like that again.'

She gave a soft laugh.

'Gods help us when you do actually screw him.'

'That's not happening,' I said firmly. 'It won't help either of us when I leave-' I broke off and she turned to me.

'When you leave? Do you still not believe you can win this?'

Trust nobody. The voice from the Atlas garden rattled through my mind.

'Well, nothing is certain,' I said evasively.

'Hmmm,' she said, and turned back to the cocktails.

I needed to change the subject again.

'So what about you? Do you have anyone that makes your brain go wonky?'

She sighed heavily and I frowned. That hadn't been the reaction I'd expected.

'Persy, I'm gonna tell you something,' she said, bringing two full glasses back to the couch.

'OK.'

'You know when I told you that I had hundreds of lovers?'

'Yeah.'

'That was a lie.'

'OK,' I said, cocking my head at her.

'I don't have any lovers.'

'Then why lie?'

'Because I don't have any lovers, ever. And never have.' She took a long swig of her drink, looking away from me.

'Oh,' I said, trying to hide my surprise.

'People judge me when they find out I'm celibate, so I lie.' Her tone was defensive and my mind churned into gear, trying to imagine what a life without sex would be like. I mean, I wasn't exactly an expert, but it had certainly livened up the last few years of my life, even if the guys had been temporary.

But that was my life, and Hecate must have her reasons for not wanting sex.

'Who the hell am I to judge you?' I said to her. 'You choose what to do with your body.' She glanced at me, her eyes more emotional than I'd seen them before.

'I wish it was my damned choice,' she muttered.

'It's not?' I frowned.

'It's complicated.' Her easy cool was returning now, and she leaned back into the couch, hooking her ankle over her other knee and sipping from her drink. 'One of my more unpleasant powers is necromancy,' she said. An involuntary shudder took me at the thought. Zombies had always scared the shit out of me. 'In an ideal world,' she continued, 'I would never have to use that power. But in the event of a cataclysmic fuck up it might be extremely important. Because, out of all the gods, only Hades and I can do it. Thanatos and the Fates can incite actual death, but we're the only ones who can animate corpses and control the souls of the dead.' I worked hard to keep the revulsion from my face.

'What kind of fuck up would require you to do that?'

She let out a long breath.

'Hades losing control of the Underworld. Or being removed from Olympus completely. The undead are one of the few things that could topple the gods.'

My breath caught. Hades removed from Olympus... Was that god-speak for him dying? I thought he was immortal?

'Could... Could that happen?'

'In Olympus, anything could happen,' she said a little bitterly. I took a steadying gulp of my cocktail.

'So you're his back up?'

'Kind of, yeah. And a power that dark must be balanced out. Hades has sacrificed parts of his own soul, physically lost pieces of himself to the Underworld. He is too strong, the demands on his power too high for him to live any other way. But for me, I learned that I could make a personal sacrifice, and keep my soul intact.'

'So you gave up sex?'

'I was a virgin when I came here, and physical love was what I wanted most back then. It was the greatest sacrifice I could make to save my soul.'

'But you didn't give up love? Just sex?'

'Persy, point me at a man who will love you without touching you,' she said, and this time her voice was full of bitterness. 'And besides, why put myself through the temptation? Why fall in love with someone and never be able to physically express it? The moment I gave in and lost my virginity, I would lose my most valuable power.'

'Shit,' I said quietly.

'Yeah.'

'But what if you never need to use that power? Surely Hades isn't going anywhere, he's like one of the super-gods isn't he?'

'Hades is the most volatile of them all. We can never know what might happen in the future. That's like weighing up my desire for a good time against the possible destruction of the whole of Olympus,' she said, looking disdainfully at me. 'Not really a risk worth taking.'

I blew out a sigh.

'Well, I hope Olympus knows what you're giving up for them,' I said. Hecate snorted.

'Do they fuck. I'm Titan scum as far as they're concerned.'

'Then why do you do it?'

'Persy, I may have an attitude problem, but I'm not going to risk watching the world fall to the undead when I could have stopped it. I told you, Titans aren't genocidal anymore.' She gave me a wry smile. 'Besides, there's no-one I want to screw that much anyway.'

By the time Hecate flashed me back to my own room, I was hammered. Like properly, well and truly, drunk. After her big revelation, and my admitting my confused feelings for Hades, the conversation had turned to lighter topics. Hecate had demanded to hear every awful and embarrassing encounter I'd ever had with a man, and Skop had provided a number of highly entertaining anecdotes too. We'd talked about what dicks Zeus and Poseidon were, and the bitching had felt good.

'You know what, Skop,' I called, as I pulled off my leather trousers in my washroom.

'You've changed your mind and want to try out gnome knob?' he answered hopefully.

'No. I was just thinking that maybe I need to see

Hades.' I pulled on the silk nightwear that always appeared clean in my wardrobe every evening, stumbling as I stepped into the little shorts.

'That's because you're drunk and randy,' he said.

'Well, some people don't get to have sex at all. I should be grateful. I should make the most of it.' In my inebriated state, this seemed like the most sensible statement I'd ever made. Why deny myself when I didn't have to? Especially to a freaking god. 'Now, how do I make him come here?'

NINETEEN

HADES

'You know what you are?' I bellowed, power bursting from the end of my pointed finger. Zeus smiled lazily back at me as he flicked his hand up and blocked it. He needn't have. He was easily strong enough to absorb my outbursts.

'What am I, Hades?'

'You're a colossal fucking prick, just as she said you were!'

Danger danced in my brother's eyes.

'I had no idea she was going to provide this much entertainment when I brought her back,' he said, strolling to the edge of my throne room and peering down at the endless flames. Rage was thundering through my body, that dark well of power desperate to expend itself.

'Zeus, without me, Olympus will fall. Do you really think putting me in my place is worth that risk?' I hissed, trying to calm myself.

'Is that a threat?' he said, raising his eyebrows as he

turned to me. He was in his true form, as was I. Ancient and glowing with the barely containable power of the sky, his face was lined with as much fury as I felt. 'You caused this, Hades. You broke the laws. You deliberately defied me. Did you expect me to let you humiliate me and belittle my rules in front of the world?' Lethal rage dripped from his words, and I felt the smoke pouring from my skin as I glared back at him.

'You killed them all. An entire innocent realm, save one. Was that not punishment enough? Did you really need to risk bringing her back just to see me suffer?'

His eyes narrowed.

'So you share Poseidon's belief that she is still dangerous?'

'She can't stay here.'

'I'm well aware of that.'

'So now you are forcing her into a Trial where my own realm will kill her? Do you despise me that much?' The smoke rolling off me was starting to burn, flames dripping like liquid from my body onto the marble floor.

'She's stronger than you think, Hades.'

'That's what your wife said,' I snarled. Zeus didn't deserve Hera. He never had. His eyes flashed with purple lightning, and the roar of thunder rumbled through the floating throne room.

'We're not talking about my wife, brother, we are talking about yours.'

'You need me, Zeus. Remember that. Sky, Sea and Underworld. If any of those three fall, Olympus falls. And then who will you have to rule over?'

'You, dear brother, are immortal. Where the fuck do you think you could go that I wouldn't find you?' He flashed and reappeared inches from my face. His fierce electricity burned through my body and jet black magic coursed through my veins in response. My monster was wide awake and ready to unleash hell. 'Desert the Underworld and I will make your life even more miserable than it has been for centuries,' he hissed.

He thought I was threatening to leave? I barked out a laugh.

'You have me all wrong, Zeus. All wrong. I won't leave Virgo. Ever. I will remain here until there is nothing left. All of Olympus will burn around me, the undead will flood the world, drowning the living with their rotting corpses, and I will be here, exactly where you put me.' *Alone. Broken, twisted and unable to contain the darkness inside me any longer.*

For the briefest of seconds I saw doubt flicker across my brother's face. But then it was gone, a smug sneer twisting his features instead. He folded his arms and stepped back from me, tilting his head.

'That is quite a threat.'

'It's not a threat. It is the consequence of pushing me too far.'

'Are you telling me that you are unstable, little brother?'

'No, Zeus,' I lied. 'I am as in control of my power as I have ever been. But I would advise you not to test me.'

He regarded me a moment longer, then sighed.

'We shall see how your little human fares tomorrow.

Her Trials are no more dangerous than those the other contestants experienced.'

'Bullshit,' I snapped. He smiled at me.

'See you tomorrow, brother,' he said, and vanished.

I roared, and the room lit up with flames.

They crawled over the dais, and I felt the darkness building inside me as they reached my throne, the skulls flaring blue as the fire touched them.

Then a shaft of light pierced my own skull, and my rage skittered as my focus shifted. *Persephone*. It was her light, her magic. I closed my eyes and sent my senses through the palace, seeking her green flare. And there it was. In her rooms. Why was she using her magic now? Was she just practicing? Or had whomever left that doll on her doorstep managed to get inside? The thought was enough to re-trigger my rage, and I flashed myself to her side instantly.

'Woooah, you look really mad,' she said as I whipped my head around the small room, looking for the threat.

'What?' I focused on her, my instincts telling me nothing dangerous was here, but my heart was pounding all the same. 'Why...' I trailed off. She was wearing a pink silk vest and shorts, and her white hair was loose around her shoulders. Her pupils were dilated, and I could smell cherries. 'Have you been drinking?' I asked her slowly.

'Spartan spirits.'

'I thought I recognized the smell,' I said, and let the smoke fade from around me, feeling my racing pulse start to slow. 'Hecate's cocktails are lethal, you know.'

'Ah, but it turns out that my new powers can heal hangovers,' she said, excitement in her slightly slurred voice. 'Which is just about the best news I've had since coming here.' I couldn't help the smile that was tugging at my mouth. She was happy. I wanted nothing more than to see her happy. Well, maybe there was one thing I wanted as much... My eyes dipped to the low neckline of her silk top.

'What were you using your magic for?' I asked her.

'I, um, wanted to see you. But I kinda broke the dresser.' She gestured to her dressing table, which was splintered completely in two. I raised my eyebrows.

'Magic wielding whilst drunk is never advisable,' I told her, and flicked my wrist. The dark wood of the dressing table began to knit itself back together.

'Why not if you can just fix whatever I mess up?' Her words, though meant teasingly, were far, far too close to home. How I wished I could fix everything.

'Well, I'm not going to fix your mess for free,' I said, folding my arms, and shoving the dark thoughts down. I was here now, and she wanted my company. I couldn't turn that down, no matter how much power was still swirling dangerously close to the surface of my skin.

'Oh yeah? What do you charge for dressing table repairs?'

'I want to see you,' I said, dropping my voice and locking my eyes on hers. She gulped.

'You can see me,' she said.

'I want to see all of you.' Her pale skin colored but she held my gaze.

'Are you trying to take advantage of my drunkenness?' she said, pronouncing each word carefully.

'Isn't that why you wanted me to come here?'

Her eyes dipped from mine and I knew I was right. She wanted me as much as I wanted her, the gold vines had shown me that. But she didn't feel the bond yet. She didn't feel the dying cord that had crackled back to life when I had seen her in my throne room, and had been glowing a tiny bit brighter every day since. I would know if she felt it too. It would burst into life, safe and solid and present and eternal.

'It might have,' she said, and swayed on her bare feet.

'I'll tell you what,' I said, my anger from earlier now merging with my arousal, pent up energy crashing around inside me like an ocean storm. I couldn't take her like this.

But there was no fucking way I was leaving with nothing.

I flicked my hand and the kobaloi barked as a smoky bubble enveloped him. I wasn't sharing this view.

'Let me see you, and maybe I'll do the same.'

TWENTY

PERSEPHONE

I raised my eyebrows as Hades stood before me, his words reverberating around my fuzzy brain.

'I'll show you mine and you show me yours?' I said, staring at him. He was so beautiful. The strong lines of his jaw, his sharp cheekbones and angular nose, the dark stubble - it was like he had been designed with as much 'man' as was available from the ingredients.

'Yes. I'll show you mine, if you show me yours.' A wicked smile was pulling at his lips and his silver eyes were dark.

'Seriously? Like we're teenagers?'

'Yes. And I guarantee I'll ruin any memory you have of anything you saw as a teenager. Or since.' I gulped. I didn't doubt it.

I wasn't exactly shy when it came to be being nude, but he was Hades, King of the Underworld. Did one just strip casually in front of an all-powerful god?

But my word, did I want to see him without those jeans on.

The thought had my hands moving before I could stop them, and I slowly drew the thin straps of my camisole off my shoulders. Without them to hold the top up, it slid down to my hips, catching on the little shorts and leaving my breasts and stomach completely exposed. I kept my eyes on his, drinking in his change in expression as his eyes raked over me. My nipples hardened as desire pulsed through my body. The all-powerful god wanted me, and it couldn't be more obvious. Or confidence-inducing. I let a coy smile dance over my lips as I ran my fingers inside the waistband of my shorts, delighting in how his breath quickened.

'I think it's your turn to lose a shirt,' I breathed. His black shirt dissolved instantly, the hard planes of his abs utterly perfect, his huge shoulders and the V of his stomach prompting shivers of pleasure through me. *Please don't drool, please don't drool,* I chanted drunkenly in my head as I pictured those divine arms lifting me, my legs wrapping around his solid waist.

I inched the shorts down.

His hand moved to the top button of his dark jeans.

Yes. Yes. Unbutton the jeans.

I wiggled my hips, easing the shorts down further. He deftly undid the first button, then the next. I realized with a small moan that he wasn't wearing underwear. Another couple of buttons, and I would see *him*.

My hands began to shake as I moved one side of the shorts down another inch.

. . .

A resounding crash from outside my room snapped both our attentions to the bedroom door, my lust and booze addled brain protesting wildly at the sudden interruption. But before I could even consider what to do next, Hades had shifted into something unrecognizable.

He grew in size, muscles bulging, electric blue light glowing from him, and I saw his face, twisted with unbridled fury before he whirled around. My bedroom door blew apart as he raised his arms, black smoke shooting from him in curling tendrils and snaking through the open door.

'You won't escape me this time,' he hissed, and his voice was like knives slicing through flesh. *Who was out there?*

A distant screaming began to grow louder in my ears, and the tang of blood crept into my nostrils as the temperature plummeted.

No, I could stop his power affecting me, I thought as I hoisted my top back up. I dug deep inside me, hunting for my power, trying to drag it up to the surface. Vines slowly emerged from my palms as Hades stalked to the door, following after his streams of smoke. The vines were gold, and they only grew about ten inches, but a light seemed to emanate from them, and the blood and the screams died away.

'Well done, vines,' I muttered, and hurried after Hades.

He had stopped in the doorway, and was standing

frozen, still pulsing with blue light and dark smoke. I ducked under his arm and stepped out into the corridor. There, against the rocky wall, was a huge broken mirror. I frowned as I looked into it. I couldn't see Hades behind me. Just my own reflection, skin flushed and silky night-wear disheveled, the image distorted by the many cracks.

'What-' I started to ask, but my words caught in my throat. I was bleeding. Scarlet red blood was seeping from my reflection's eyes. Nausea rose in my gut and my hands flew to my face, my vines brushing my cheeks as I touched them. I looked down at my fingers. There was nothing. But... When I looked back at my reflection it wasn't just my eyes that were bleeding. Blood poured from me, my skin cracking like the glass in front of me, the thick ooze gushing onto the floor.

Words began to appear across the mirror. 'You will drown in the river of blood you created.'

I stumbled backwards, starting when I hit something ice cold and solid. I whirled, tearing my eyes from the hideous mirror and staring up into Hades' furious eyes.

He was almost harder to look at than the mirror was. His beautiful features were torn and ragged, his eyes filled with black fire, the silver gone completely. Pure fury poured from him, and I could see the shapes of bodies forming in the blue light around him. Screams crept back into my ears, primal fear trickling through my whole body and forcing me to step back from him. His rage-fueled power this close up was too strong for my defenses.

'I will destroy whomever is doing this,' he snarled.

'Death is too good for them. They will burn for all eternity.'

'You're scaring me, Hades,' I said, trying to keep the growing terror from my voice. He fixed his eyes on mine, and they were almost black now. He gripped me by my shoulders, lifting me bodily off my feet and turned, depositing me back in my room. His touch was ice cold and visions of corpses littering the ground flew through my head until he let go.

'I must go,' he said, his voice hard as stone. With a flash he was gone, my bedroom door shimmering back into existence.

I stared at it, my whole body shuddering as my vines vanished. Bile burned hot and acidic in my throat, the cocktails now seeming like a very bad idea. I held my hand up to the wood of the door, feeling its sturdiness. Was the mirror still there, on the other side?

'I hope he gets the bastards. You know, if he didn't keep blocking me out I might have been able to help,' said Skop. His voice was hard too. Warmth was beginning to seep back over me now, and I dropped my hand, taking a step away from the door. The shaking was easing.

'Did you see the mirror?' I asked quietly.

'No. What happened?'

I told the kobaloi what I had seen in the glass, as I poured myself some water and sat down on my bed.

'Who is doing this?'

'Hades will find out,' Skop said reassuringly, jumping up beside me.

'What if I deserve it?' I asked, voicing the question I

was finding so hard to bury deep enough to ignore. 'What if I did cause rivers of blood?'

'You *were born twenty-six years ago, in New York.* You *didn't do anything,*' he said gently.

I let his words comfort me. He was right. Whatever old Persephone did, I didn't know if I would be capable of the same.

Old Persephone had loved Hades. And if I had forgotten it, tonight had reminded me - the King of the Underworld had a monster inside him.

I stayed there on my bed, alert and on edge, for more than an hour before I heard from Hades. My whirring mind was racing through morbid ideas of what I might have done in my previous life, when a tentative voice sounded inside my head.

'*Persephone?*'

'Hades!'

'*I'm sorry, but they got away this time.*' I felt my shoulders droop with disappointment. '*I want you to stay in your room until Hecate comes for you tomorrow. And no more conservatory or training room visits alone.*' His steely voice gave no room for argument, and although I knew what he said made sense, I bristled at the idea of not being able to visit the conservatory by myself.

'What about Skop?' I asked. There was a long pause.

'*When Dionysus volunteered the sprite as a guard, I don't believe he actually thought you would need defending from any threats. Skoptolis is not equipped to deal with this. He can stay with you, of course, but when I say alone, I mean without Hecate, a member of my guard, or me.'*

I let out a long breath.

'OK. Do you think whoever is doing this will try to hurt me?' He didn't answer, and a little trickle of fear coiled through my chest. 'Fine. I'll add this to the list of things I need to survive,' I said, trying to mask the fear with my casual words, and failing.

'The next Trial is an intelligence test. You'll do great. But I would like to apologize in advance.'

'For what?'

'I strongly suspect you're going to see some of the worst the Underworld has to offer tomorrow.' The tension in his voice made me realize how hard that must be for him. His own realm was going to be used against me.

'I have my magic back. Have you seen those black vines? I'll kick the ass of anything your crappy Virgo throws at me,' I announced as loftily as I could. He didn't laugh, but when he next spoke his voice was soft.

'I don't doubt it, Beautiful.'

My forced bravado deserted me once I was lying in bed though, trying and failing to sleep. Skop's reassuring presence at my feet helped, but not enough to dispel the disappointment that Hades hadn't caught the culprit, or the constant wondering about whether I deserved the awful gifts.

Eventually exhaustion pulled me into an uneasy sleep, and I tossed and turned until I heard the faint sound of birdsong. Slowly, it got louder, and I stepped gratefully out of the darkness of my sleep-induced imagination into the Atlas garden.

'Do you know who is sending me these messages?' I asked almost immediately, inhaling the earthy scent of the stunning garden gratefully.

'I do not. But I do know that you should not rely on Hades to fix this for you.'

'What do you mean?'

'You are gaining your power back, Little Goddess. One more seed and you will be able to deal with them yourself.'

I knelt and ran my hand through moist soil, the feeling of it on my skin like home.

'But I don't know who it is or how to find them, or even why they are doing it. They say I am a murderer.'

'You have been wrongly blamed for their losses. Regain your memories, and oust the true villain. That is the only way you shall find freedom from this.'

'You said I would know where the river Lethe was when I got more power back. But I don't.'

'Then you must win more seeds, and gain more power.'

I nodded. Maybe it was time to eat the last seed.

TWENTY-ONE

PERSEPHONE

The next morning though, as I stared into the little box with the last magically preserved pomegranate seed in it, I couldn't do it. I couldn't pick one up and put it my mouth, no matter how much sense it made to me.

'*What's the problem?*' asked Skop impatiently, sat on the floor beside my dressing table stool.

'I don't know,' I said, staring at my reflection. But I did. The longer I looked at myself, the more sure I was that I could see tears the color of blood, leaking from my eyes and down my face. The image from that mirror, my skin cracking and rotting, the blood pouring from me... I knew for certain that the person I was now couldn't be responsible for causing rivers of blood. But I didn't know for certain what more power would do to me. They could turn me back into that person. I had vines that tried to steal another's magic. That seemed pretty dark to me. It was *wrong*.

Power corrupts. This was something I knew to be true. The kids with the most influence and strength at school had always been the cruelest. And the longer they stayed at the top of the pack, the nastier they became, pushing and testing the limits of their popularity. And that could only be worse in a place like Olympus. Hecate had told me how Hades had needed to lose parts of his soul in order to use his power to rule the Underworld.

I was caught in a desperate loop. In order to find out if the powerful Persephone had done something truly terrible, I needed to gain more power.

'The damned irony,' I sighed.

'You might need more magic for the Trial today,' Skop said.

'It's an intelligence test. I don't think I need more magic right now,' I said, tearing my eyes form the warping reflection in front of me and standing up. 'What I need is a shower and something to eat.'

After washing and dressing in my leather fighting garb, I found a pile of bacon the size of my head and a large wedge of warm bread on the dresser. I devoured it, absently noting that I may not have the headache and nausea of a hangover, but I sure had the appetite.

'So what do you think I can expect today?' I asked Skop.

'I don't know Virgo well enough to have any clue,' he said. *'They'd better not use me as bait again, or I'll be having words with Dionysus,'* he grumbled.

'I'm sure they won't,' I said, not really sure at all.

'*I do know there are some pretty ugly demons here.*'

'Ugly I can handle,' I said around my breakfast. 'What's the worst?'

'*Cerberus,*' he said, without hesitation. '*I like dogs, but he's a scary bastard.*'

'Well, I highly doubt I'll be meeting him today.'

'*Yeah, it does seem a bit early in the competition,*' he nodded.

'What? You mean I might actually meet him at some point?'

'*Well, yeah. If you're going to live here, then you'll have to test your strength against Hades personal hell-hound at some point.*' I gaped at him.

'Shit,' I said eventually.

'*But I doubt you'll have to worry about that for a while. And Charybdis is one of Poseidon's worst monsters, and you survived him.*'

I gave him a sideways glare.

'Don't remind me,' I muttered. I was still bitter that I'd won no seeds. Plus, I sort of wanted to see Buddy the hippocampus again.

'*Yeah, he's like a giant asshole with teeth,*' the dog said, and gave a little shudder. '*I wouldn't want to be reminded of almost being sucked into that either.*'

'You're gross,' I told him.

A knock at my door made us both look up, and Hecate pushed it open.

'I heard what happened last night,' she said as soon as she came in. 'You OK?'

'I'm fine,' I told her. 'I just wish I knew who was doing it. First the doll, then the mirror... Hades seems worried they'll step it up.' Her face was hard, and with all her sharp silver jewelry and black leather I was reminded of how intimidating she was when we first met in the cave.

'They want to hope they die before Hades or I get hold of them,' she said, and a mix of fear and gratitude rolled through me.

'I don't want anyone else to die because of me,' I said quickly.

'Trespassing in Virgo, particularly in the palace, is punishable by death,' she said shortly.

'Palace?' It had never occurred to me that we were in a palace.

'Yeah. We're in the palace above the business part of the Underworld.'

'And the 'business part' is where we're going for the Trial today?' *And where the river Lethe must be,* I thought.

'Yes.'

'Do dead people actually live in the Underworld?'

'Sort of. It's complicated. Souls are the only part of the dead that live on, and they don't take up any space.'

'But you said yesterday that the undead could rise.'

'You can get bodies from anywhere.' I cringed at her words, but tried to stay on track.

'So what else is in the 'business part'?'

Hecate cocked her head at me, then sighed.

'OK, super fast lesson in the Underworld. Souls go to one of three places; Elysium and the Isles of the Blessed if they led an exceptional life, the Mourning Fields if they led a life of unrequited love, and the rest go to the Asphodel Meadows. The Underworld also houses Tartarus the torture prison, lots of very cranky demons and species that are essential to Olympus but too unpleasant to live out in the world, and a bunch of rivers.'

I blinked at her.

'That's quite a lot of stuff.'

'Yeah.'

'How many rivers are there?'

'That's your question? Not *what sort of unpleasant demons*, or, *why is there a whole place for unrequited love souls*, but *how many rivers?*'

I shrugged.

'I like water,' I said lamely.

'Well these rivers aren't made of water and will all kill you. There are five, and they are sentient deities in their own right. For example, the river Styx circles the Underworld seven times and is made of hatred. And you want to stay the fuck away from her.'

'How can something be made of hatred?'

'If you become Queen you'll learn all about all the rivers. But they are not going to be the subject of today's Trial, as you couldn't be trapped in any of them without dying instantly so let's move on.'

'Fine,' I sighed. 'Tell me about the unpleasant demons instead.'

'I'm in charge of a bunch of them, and they're all

assholes,' she muttered. 'Keres demons, for example, are the deities of violent death. Arae are demons of curses, Lamia are rotten vampiric demons who drink blood, as are Empusa but they're usually on fire too. Then you've got a couple of really nasty spirits, like Eurynomos, who is the demon of rotting corpses, and the three Furies, who are goddesses of vengeance and need seriously reining in most of the time. And then you've got some who are just weird, like Ceuthonymos, who's a spirit we can never pin down and haunts anyone who's not a Titan.'

'Right,' I breathed, forgetting completely about the river. 'Do you think I'm going to meet any of them today?'

'Maybe, yes. You've got *Faesforos*?' I patted my thigh as I nodded. 'Good. I made you that blade because it can be used against any foe. And that includes Underworld demons.'

'And I'm extremely grateful,' I told her. My nerves were beginning to hum. Blood drinking vampires and demons of rotting corpses? The Spartae skeleton was starting to seem pretty tame right now. 'This is an intelligence test though, right? I hopefully won't be fighting.'

'Fingers crossed,' she answered, without a trace of hope in her voice, and a half-assed smile.

She flashed us to Hades' throne room, and my eyes shot to his throne immediately, instinctively. He was there, smoky and translucent, and he gave me the briefest flash of silver eyes. Energy pulsed through me, and I rocked on the balls of my booted feet as I scanned along the row of gods. To my astonishment, Poseidon tipped his head to me as I made eye contact with him.

'Good day, Olympus!' sang the commentator's voice, and he glimmered into the space between me and the gods. 'Today Persephone will be facing one of Hecate's creations. She will need to escape the Empusa's lair!' I glanced at Hecate and wished I hadn't. Her face was a mask of dismay.

'Empusa? Please tell me that's not the vampire who's usually on fire?' I hissed to her, pulse now racing.

'Erm,' she whispered, her eyes filled with apology. But before she could say anything else, the room flashed white around me.

TWENTY-TWO

PERSEPHONE

The first thing I noticed was the smell. Sweet rotten meat and moldy earth swamped my nostrils and I was gagging before the light even cleared from my eyes.

'What the-' I started to say, but trailed off as I looked around me. I was standing in the middle of a cave, but unlike the rocky walls that glowed with daylight that I'd seen in Virgo so far, these walls glowed deep red. And they were casting their light over a floor littered with bones.

My stomach roiled as I gaped around at the room. Rows of alcoves were gouged into the rocky walls and there were hundreds of tiny figures lining them, made of something pale and ivory colored. More bone, I realized, as I stepped closer to the wall, screwing my face up as something crunched and sludged beneath my boots. *Don't throw up, don't throw up,* I chanted in my head, as a fresh wave of putridness assaulted my senses. I tried to remember the smell of meadow flowers and lavender and lilies and incredibly, the rotting smell faded a little, and I was sure I actually *could* smell lavender. Was that my powers?

Able to concentrate slightly better now, I pulled my attention from the rows of bone carvings to the rest of the small room. The thing that had caused all this must be in here somewhere. And so must a way out. All the walls looked completely solid though, and the room was only fifty feet around. All I could see on the floor were the remains of the prey of whatever lived here.

'Hello?' I called out cautiously, scanning the rocky walls for any clues to what I was supposed to do.

'Good day,' issued a silky voice, and I froze.

'Erm, where are you?'

A figure shimmered into being before me and my heart did a small gallop in my chest at the sight of her. I'd seen her before, when I was very first dumped in Hades' throne room, but not this close. She was beautiful, her barely clad body curvy and voluptuous, and her face angular and grand. But her hair was made of flames. Two short sharp horns jutted up from her forehead, and as I dragged my eyes over her I saw that one of her legs was made from wood.

'I saw you when I first arrived here,' I breathed.

'No. That was one of my sisters. We are the Empusa, pawns of Hecate. Welcome to my lair.'

'Oh. Thanks, nice to meet you,' I said, nerves making my voice hitch. 'Do you know how I can get out of here? Not that it's not...' I looked around, scrabbling for something polite to say about her disgusting lair.

'I have four riddles for you,' she said, saving me the trouble. 'If you can not solve them all, then you are mine.' Two fangs shot down over her bottom lip as an evil smile settled on her face. I shuddered as two thin lines of blood trickled down her chin, from where the fangs had torn her lip. Her fiery hair flickered and danced around her head, making her skin look like it was rippling. She gestured with an elegant arm and I followed it to see four holes appearing in a shoulder height section of the rocky wall. They were just big enough to put a hand in.

'Number one. I build my home with natural string, and defend myself with bite or sting. What am I?'

A home from natural string? That had to be a spider web.

'A spider?' The Empusa stared at me, her face unchanging. Did that mean I was wrong? Fear made my chest clench at the thought. I didn't want to die at all, but being eaten by this thing and left to rot here... I'd rather have been eaten by the giant sea-asshole, Charybdis, than have trinkets carved from my bones to adorn this place.

But she didn't move, and I frowned. I was sure the answer was right. There must be more to the Trial than just answering the questions.

I looked back at the four holes in the wall. Four riddles, four holes. Were they keyholes? Keys in Olympus were weird, I already knew that from those awful hourglasses.

So maybe I needed a spider key for the first hole? As I turned back to the lair my gut churned again. Please,

please tell me I didn't have to find an actual spider. Please.

'Do I need to find a spider?' I asked the Empusa, my voice small. Her smile widened ever so slightly. Bile rose in my throat as I looked at the nearest heap of bones on the floor.

Then my eyes flicked to the rows of carvings. Was there one carved as a spider? I moved to the nearest wall quickly, and heard a deep rumble. A soft, sensual laugh bubbled from the Empusa's mouth and I looked at her.

'You'd better hurry, pretty little human,' she said, her eyes filled with glee.

A new smell hammered at the lavender barrier I'd somehow concocted. *Sewage.* My gut constricted, causing me to retch as I swept my eyes over the room fast. Where was it coming from? A gurgling sound dragged my attention to the floor, and my pulse quickened as I saw a black sludge starting to ooze up from the ground, thick enough to displace the rotting bones.

'What is that?'

'Your doom,' the flame-haired demon grinned at me.

I didn't wait to find out what she meant. If I had four riddles to get through I didn't have time to let the sludge get any higher. I raced along the shelves, scanning every little carving, looking for a spider.

'Yes!' I hissed as I finally spotted a tiny bone carving in the shape of a spider, and reached out for it. As I picked it up though, heat burned through my finger tips, and I saw a flash of fire and blood. I yelped as I dropped it back on the shelf.

Another soft laugh came from the Empusa and I turned to glare at her.

'You are no creature of the Underworld. You may not touch my treasures, human.'

'I'm not entirely human any more,' I snapped, nerves humming as I hesitantly called up my vines. Relief washed through me when a green shoot began to ease gently from my right palm. The black vines were absolutely not what I needed right now. They tended to fly about angrily all over the place, and I definitely did not want to knock any of these carvings into the rising sludge. It was oozing over the toes of my boots now, and it reeked. Plus, if the black vines really did steal power like Hades said they did, the last thing I wanted was any of this Empusa's power inside me. *Yuk.*

I directed the vine towards the toppled spider carving, but as it got close it veered away, almost like when you try to put the wrong end of two magnets together. I concentrated, forcing the vine back towards it. But as it touched the bone, revulsion swamped me, the total opposite of the joy I felt when I connected with the earth and living plants. My breakfast rose fast in my stomach, and I snapped the vine away, heaving again.

'Life and death, light and dark... You will not master the balance,' the Empusa hissed. I looked up at her, sweat now trickling down my neck.

'Black vines it is then,' I hissed back, and a dark vine

shot from my palm, smashing into the row of carvings. 'Shit!' I yelped, trying to control the whipping shoot. *Get your shit together Persephone, unless you want to drown in sewage,* I berated myself. With an effort, I pulled back the black vine, then sent it carefully towards the spider. Gingerly, slowly, I managed to wrap the vine around the bone carving.

A new, dark energy hummed along the vine and into my hand, spreading through my veins like fire. I saw no awful images, felt no searing heat, but I knew on every level that the power was wrong. It was fueled by fear and blood, and it didn't belong inside me. My whole damned body was sweating now, nerves and stress and fear pumping more adrenaline through me.

I could feel my temper rising, anger starting to simmer deep inside me as I hurried over to the four holes in the wall, the spider carving wrapped in my vine. The sludge was covering my boots completely now, and was half way up my shins. I found that lifting my feet out of it allowed me to move faster than trying to move through it; it was as thick as tar.

When I reached the wall, I carefully lowered the spider into the first hole, and willed the vine to let go. As it did a small click sounded, then rock began to fill the hole, growing all the way out of the wall and forming a small handle.

'Thank fuck for that,' I muttered, half panting as the brimming anger inside me abated. I gripped the handle, and discovered I could only turn it left ninety degrees, so that's what I did before turning back to the Empusa.

'Number two. My golden treasure never lacks a guard, and is held in a maze from which men are barred. What am I?'

'Golden treasure?' It had to be an animal of some sort, I thought looking at the carvings. My mind whirred, trying to think of an animal that had golden treasure. I didn't even know about half the animals in Olympus, so I'd have to hope we had the same animals in my world. What had gold treasure in a maze? 'A bee!' I shouted, as the answer came to me. I dragged my legs through the sludge, and started hunting through the shelves.

If I survived this, I was showering for a week. It took me until the sludge had reached my waist to find the fucking bee carving. The stench was becoming unbearable, my magical lavender no match for its ferocity. I carried the bee carefully over to the holes in the wall, my progress infuriatingly slow, and anger roiling inside me the whole time my black vine was cradling the carving. It was toxic, I was sure. The second I connected with the bones I could feel their dark, angry influence. I tipped the carving into the next hole as soon as I reached it and the hole filled in quickly, a second handle forming. I yanked it up and turned back to the Empusa, knowing I must have a wretched scowl on my face.

Just get it done. Just get it done. You'll be out of here soon.

The dark red light, the awful stench, the oppressive heat, the nauseating bones surrounding me; all were making the fury building inside me harder to dispel. This place was a damned hell-hole, and once again I was suffering for those bastard gods' entertainment. I needed to get out, before I lost my shit, which would almost definitely result in my death.

This wasn't an intelligence test, I thought bitterly. It was a test of temper.

'Number three. Although I only have two eyes on my head, my tail has a magnificent spread. What am I?'

I snarled in anger. There was nothing in my world that had a spread of eyes on its tail. How was I supposed to find something if I didn't even know what I was looking for?

But I had barely stamped towards the nearest shelf before I paused, my eyes snagging on a carving of what looked like a parrot. I'd seen other birds when I was looking for the last two carvings, and my mind flashed to the feather on Hera's mask at the masquerade ball.

'A peacock,' I exclaimed, and moved as fast as I could through the rising ooze to where I thought I'd seen the bird carvings. Sure enough, after a little hunting, I wrapped my vine around a detailed peacock carving. It was getting easier to control the vine, but harder to subdue the surge of rage that accompanied contact with the awful carvings. I made my way to the holes as fast as I could, but it was like I was wading through quicksand, and any speed was impossible. The sludge was higher than my waist. When I finally dropped the peacock into the third hole there was a click, then the rock morphed slowly into a third handle.

Just one left, I thought, pulling up the handle then balling my fists. One more stinking, rotten, vile carving left to find, and I was out of here.

'Last, but not least,' the Empusa said, and something about her sinister expression made my skin crawl. 'I have the head of a leopard, the middle of a pig, the rear of a flamingo and the tail of a dragon. What am I?'

I stared at her. Surely there was no creature in Olympus that fit that description. Surely. The rear of a flamingo and the tail of a freaking dragon?

'The ugliest damned thing in the world?' I hissed, raking through my brain to come up with an answer. Wasn't a chimera what the Greeks had called a monster made up of other animals? But that was made of an eagle and a lion or something, not flamingos and pigs.

Panic was beginning to prick at my forced calm. I had to answer this right. My life depended on it. I could feel my power under the skin of my hands, humming with need, longing to break free of my fragile control.

Come on, Persy, it's an intelligence test, not a Greek mythology test. There was no way that creature exists, I reasoned. Which meant it had to be a trick question, or a different kind of riddle. The head of a leopard. Did that mean spots? Middle of a pig might mean pink? As were flamingos... A pink spotty thing with a dragon tail?

Another bark of frustration escaped me. Head,

middle, rear and tail. Did that equate to start, middle and end? The start of leopard was 'L'. The middle of pig was 'I'. My heart raced as I thought through the riddle. Rear of a flamingo could mean the last letter, which was 'O' and if the tail of a dragon meant the same thing that was an 'N'.

'Lion!' I shouted the word, and this time the smile on the Empusa's face faltered. She hadn't wanted me to work it out.

With renewed vigor I forced my way through the stinking sludge, now almost at my shoulders, looking fervently for anything resembling a lion. Eventually, on a shelf almost too high for me to see, I spotted a carving with what looked like the ring of a mane around it. I sent my vine up towards it, and when the shoot made contact, I swear I could hear an actual lion roaring. All my muscles clenched as the dark, greedy, angry power flooded through me.

Kill her. Kill the vampire bitch.

The words were in my own voice, in my own head, but they didn't belong to me.

Fuck these riddles, these games, kill the demon.

The world whirled around me as darkness burned through my body, black and hot and brutal. I stared dumbly at the lion carving as images of my vines wrapping around the Empusa, dousing her stupid hair in the sewage, tearing her wooden leg away... A wave of sweet, rotting stench invaded my nostrils, mercifully snapping me out of the brutal vision.

The smell had been caused by the sewage reaching my neck, now only inches from my nose, I realized with a start. I heaved once more as I turned, hardly able to pull myself through the ooze now. Holding the lion carving high, fury and fear making my limbs shake, I lifted my other arm out of the thick black stuff, and fired a vine from my free hand at the handles on the wall. The vine smashed into one of them, and I willed the vine to curl around it.

Just as the sludge edged over my jaw and reached my mouth, I yanked, instructing the vine to retract, and take me with it. I was instantly pulled off my feet, the force of the vine tugging me through the disgusting sewage. It splattered around my face, and my eyes streamed with the acridity of it, but the vine pulled me on, and my head stayed above the surface.

But when I smashed into the wall, I realized with horror that the last hole was submerged. I plunged my hand into the rising muck, feeling frantically for it, but it was too deep.

I would have to put my head under.

A fresh surge of hatred for the people who had put me in here and forced me through this rose inside me and I very nearly smashed the lion carving against the wall in fury.

But I retracted the vine at the last second, rational thoughts forcing their way through the red mist. *Put the lion in the hole and it's over!*

With a huge breath, I closed my eyes and let myself drop through the heavy sludge.

It was so thick that I instantly panicked, the feeling of being crushed overwhelming. I scrabbled at the wall with my free hand, feeling for the handles to work my way down to the last hole. My heart was hammering so fast I thought my chest might burst, the weight around me pressing in hard, my eyes burning behind my eyelids.

I was going to die here, suffocated in sewage.

My fingers snagged on a sharp edge, and my body tried to take an involuntary breath as I realized it must be the hole. Acrid sludge burned my lips and nostrils as I drew the vine holding the lion desperately to my other hand, which was now gripping the hole. My lungs burned for air, every single instinct in my body warring with my instructions to stay calm and not breathe. I shoved the lion carving into what I prayed was the hole. The stuff was moving further up my nose, starting to fill the back of my throat, and it burned like acid. It was too much. My mouth started to open.

A handle formed under my fingers, and I yanked it.

TWENTY-THREE

HADES

I gripped the arms of my throne as Persephone appeared in the middle of the throne room floor, covered in the thick black sewage. She fell forward onto her hands and knees, heaving, and white hot fury roared in me, so close to breaking free from my godly constraints. *Look what they have done to her. They will all die.*

'Can't... breathe...' her words were ragged, and I leapt from my throne, but Poseidon got there first. In a flash he was standing in front of her, a cascade of water pouring from thin air over her body. Her back arched slightly and she began to take deep, shuddering breaths. My coiled muscles relaxed ever so slightly, but I glared at the back of Poseidon's head.

Watching her drown in that shit-hole, the lair of a creature created by Hecate, her only friend here, and supplied with prey by me, had been torture. My own realm had almost killed her, and Zeus had me powerless to help her. The monster inside me was hungry, and my brother was the subject of its attentions. Had she actually died in there...

Suddenly black vines whipped from Persephone's palms and she was staggering to her feet. Her wild eyes were filled with hatred, and the vines blasted towards the thrones. Artemis, Ares and Zeus leapt to their feet as her voice roared through the room, clear and crisp and furious.

'I'm sick of this! You are done playing with me!'

Poseidon threw up his hand and spoke as Zeus and I stepped forward.

'It is the Underworld sewage making her angry. She will be fine when it has all been cleansed from her.' His gaze was fixed on Persephone as the jet of water above her tightened and moved, forming a powerful jet. The black stuff began to sluice off her drenched body, her white hair clinging to her furious face.

'Why are you helping me?' she hissed at Poseidon, the vines still flicking fiercely through the air.

'Put the vines away, Persephone,' he answered her calmly. 'I'm helping you because my hippocampus liked you.'

Her eyebrows shot up in surprise and the tension in the vines slackened immediately.

'You give a shit what a hippocampus thinks?'

'Very, very much.'

She held his gaze a moment longer, then lowered her palms. The black vines disintegrated. I let out a long breath, and backed up again, glancing sideways at the other gods who had stood up. They all followed suit,

Zeus flashing me a look that made my blood boil even hotter.

'I think it's all gone now,' Persephone said quietly, looking down at herself. All the slime had washed away. But the anger lingered on her face, hot and barely contained. I could feel it emanating from her. The shower of water stopped and Poseidon shimmered, then reappeared on his throne.

'And now to be judged!' sang the commentator, his normally irritating voice ever so slightly tense as he appeared at the foot of the dais. Persephone turned slowly on the spot, clearly knowing what to expect. The three judges, one cold, one fat and one wise, were seated behind her. *Five more minutes, Persephone, and you'll be alone. Just keep it together for five more minutes,* I willed.

'Radamanthus?'

'One token.'

'Aeacus?'

'One token.'

'And Minos?'

'I agree with my colleagues. You will be awarded one token,' Minos said. The seed box appeared in Persephone's wet hand and she stared down at it.

'There you have it, folks! With four Trials still to go, little

Persephone has won four tokens. Let's not forget that Minthe, the current leader, completed the nine Trials with a total of five tokens. Persephone only needs two more to win the position of Queen of the Underworld.'

Persephone's eyes found mine, and I could see the realization dawn on her face. She could end this in just two more trials.

'For her next Trial, tomorrow evening, our favorite little human will be facing an endurance test like no other. Of the twelve gods, four will have a surprise for her. Dress for the occasion!'

With that, the commentator vanished. I stared at the spot he had been standing in, my mind whirring. The gods had endurance tests planned for her? Well, I certainly wasn't one of four who had been selected. I threw a dirty glance at my brother and Zeus grinned back at me.

'Hades?' Persephone's voice in my mind made my whole body flinch, and as I looked at her I saw the barely contained power brimming over inside her, green light glowing from her body. 'Help me,' she whispered in my head.

I flashed to her, grabbing her burning hot hand, then flashed us both to the first place my brain connected with her. Our derelict breakfast room.

'Let it out, Persephone, you're safe here,' I told her. Something dark was dancing in her green eyes, and now her actual skin was glowing too. Vines erupted from her palms and she threw her head back as a blast of energy burst from her. The breakfast room was lined with windows fifty feet tall, and the glass smashed in every single one of them in unison.

As her power hit me I staggered slightly, not because of the strength but because of the way it felt. It wasn't just fury or wrath. There was more, something deeper. She needed to use her true power, I realized.

I moved quickly to the little platform her tree used to grow from, and made myself larger, forcing her attention onto me.

'Use the green vines. There is earth under here,' I said loudly, stamping on the cracked marble beneath my feet.

Immediately her vines turned green, bolting towards my feet. I moved fast out of the way as they smashed through the remaining tiles, churning through the hard, dead earth beneath. Then she gasped, and the green glow around her intensified.

Everything stilled to nothing as I watched my Queen, my beautiful goddess, turn the dark fury of the Underworld into awesome, unbound life.

Lightning fast, the trunk of the blossom tree began to grow from the middle of the platform, swirling and spiraling as it got larger, branches shooting from the trunk, then leaves and flowers following fast. Grass rose from the churning soil at the base, daisies sprouting amid the green turf. Pink petals began to dominate the sweeping branches as they extended over the table, and I could almost feel a phantom breeze ripple past me and through them.

Life. Color. Light.

I had longed for this tree for twenty-six years.

Her vines went slack suddenly, and she stumbled as they disintegrated. I flashed to her as her knees gave out, scooping her up and setting her down in one of the two chairs at the table. *Always laid for two but never used.* She took a shuddering breath as she looked up into my face and my heart swelled with so much hope and love that it actually rivaled the size of the dark pit of power in my gut.

I would never let her go again. I couldn't. She was light and life and love, and she was mine.

TWENTY-FOUR

PERSEPHONE

'W-what did I just do,' I stammered, staring up into Hades' intense silver eyes. He had an almost awestruck look on his face which was making me nervous, although I was too thoroughly drained for my body to react to my nerves. I could barely hold my own head up. I didn't feel like I was going to pass out though, which was something.

'You channeled your rage into earth magic. You regrew a tree that you used to keep alive here,' Hades said softly, and crouched in front of the chair he had put me in so that our eyes were level. I slowly tipped my head backwards and looked up. A pink blossom petal wafted down from the overhanging branches and landed on my wet hair. 'You used to laugh when they fell in your soup,' Hades said, his deep voice filled with emotion. I looked back at him.

'We ate in here?' He nodded. 'I knew I felt something about these chairs when I first saw them,' I muttered.

'You had them made for us. You said that there should be a place in my kingdom where I didn't have to be a king, so you made the chairs to show our powers equally. To share my burden.'

The intensity in his voice was almost too much to bear.

'Sounds like I was a pretty good wife,' I smiled, attempting to lessen the sadness. His face relaxed slightly.

'Now don't go getting an inflated opinion of yourself,' he grinned, rocking back on his heels. 'You'll start sounding like the other gods.'

His words wiped the smile from my face and he winced.

'I'm sorry. I know you must hate us all right now.'

'Hate doesn't come close,' I growled, but my burning rage from before was spent. 'Although I don't think I'm actually able to hate you. Something won't let me,' I told him.

'Even though you've just seen what my realm is made of, and it tried to kill you?'

'I don't want to live here, if that's what you're asking,' I half snorted. 'But I don't hold you responsible. I know you didn't choose to put me through this.'

'You did great, if it's any consolation. Underworld sewage is highly toxic, you would never have survived without controlling your black vines.'

'How did I change them from black to green?' I asked him. He cocked his head slightly.

'I don't know,' he admitted eventually. 'Before, if

you got angry your power was all rage. This time though, I could feel your earth magic trying to get through.'

Hope and something that might have been excitement prickled inside me.

'So I might have better control of my angry power than before?' *Did that mean it was safe to eat another seed?*

'No god ever has full control over true wrath,' he said slowly. 'I don't know how you grew the tree. But you did.'

Nor did I. I had been ready to explode, the fury poisoning me from the inside out. But when Hades had stamped on the platform, my vines had taken over and the delicious feeling of thriving life had flooded my body, flushing the hate from my system.

'Do you have anything to drink?' I asked Hades. 'I kind of had my face filled with sewage. The aftertaste is pretty unpleasant.'

'Of course,' he said, leaping to his feet. I moved myself slowly, until I was sitting up in the chair. I gazed at the intricate detail on the arms and wondered how the hell I'd ever come up with something like this. But the more I looked, the more familiar it felt. The shape of the roses, the curve of the skulls, the patterns of the vines... Maybe I *could* see that same spark of creativity that went into my garden designs here.

'This should help,' said Hades, and I dragged my eyes from the chair and took the goblet he was holding out to me. It smelled like hot chocolate but it was golden in color. I raised my eyebrows at him.

'What is it?'

'Ambrosia.'

'Hecate said humans couldn't drink this,' I said, peering at the thick liquid.

'I think you've just demonstrated that you have enough power to handle it,' he said gently. 'But go easy.'

I took a slow sip. It tasted like the richest, most luxurious hot chocolate ever. Almost like melted chocolate, rather than that shitty powder stuff.

'Oh my gods, it's gorgeous.'

'Not as gorgeous as you,' he muttered, and dropped down in front of me again. 'When you use your power like that... You look divine. It's all I can do not to tear your clothes off.'

His voice had become low and husky, and the warm drink was working its way through my chest now, my fatigue vanishing in its wake.

'Well, they are pretty messed up. And wet,' I said.

'I had noticed,' he whispered, and with a little pop, the damp fabric sticking to my skin was gone. I let out a tiny squeak as I looked down at myself. *The silk pajamas.* 'Maybe we could pick up where we left off?'

Desire danced in his eyes as he asked the question, and my body responded to him instantly. I took another slow sip of the ambrosia, warmth and energy spreading through me. I didn't know if it was the drink or the thought of Hades naked, but something was definitely revitalizing me. Tingles of excitement were rippling through me and I had a skipping feeling in my chest as Hades stood up. I stared at the beautiful god before me. He really was perfection.

I leaned forward to put the goblet on the ground, and as I straightened, I took the hem of my camisole on my fingertips.

His lips parted and his eyes darkened as he towered over me.

'You first,' I said.

His shirt was gone in an instant. It was as though he had been carved from marble, every curve and bulge of his chest screaming strength and power. My eyes were level with the waist of his low jeans, and the V of his abs dipping into the denim caused a surge of heat in my core, my muscles clenching. I reached out instinctively, desperate to touch his solid stomach, but he was just out of my reach. A tiny gold vine slid from my palm, curling towards him. I looked up into his face, unsure. He nodded.

The little vine touched his glowing skin, and merged with it, a shining gold tattoo sprawling up his ribs and across his chest.

Fierce desire exploded inside me, and before I knew what was happening I was standing, and he was lifting me and his mouth found mine. I buried my hands in his hair, with nothing in my head at all besides being as close to him as was physically possible as I wrapped my legs around him. His tongue flicked against mine and a pulse so fierce it almost hurt pounded between my legs.

'You are stunning, my Queen,' he murmured against

my skin as his lips moved down my jaw. His words should have embarrassed me, but his voice was so loaded with passion, his intent and sincerity so clear, that my core clenched tighter.

'Your Queen?' I breathed.

'My Queen,' he repeated.

'I seem to remember you saying something about worshiping me.'

'I also said something about you screaming my name when I touch you, and watching you come over and over,' he said, moving so that I could see his darkening eyes. 'What I didn't tell you, is that I'm going to make you feel so incredible you won't remember your own name. I'm going to make you feel things you didn't even know were possible to feel. I'm going to bring you to the edge of ecstasy as many times as it takes for you to beg me to let you fall. And I'm going to fall with you.' A small noise I didn't think I'd ever made before escaped my lips.

He dropped to his knees, setting me down on the chair again, and began to kiss my neck, moving down slowly. Heat rolled from him, and every time his lips touched my skin electricity fired through my body. As he reached my breasts he kissed over the thin silk of my camisole, my nipples hardening instantly. His tongue flicked over one through the fabric, and another wave of need crashed between my legs.

My thighs were still clenched around his solid waist and I gasped as I felt his hand under one of them, moving up towards my shorts. As his fingertips stroked higher I arched my back, pleasure and need making me dizzy. His fingers danced higher and higher, teasing me until I was squirming under him. I had my hands in his hair, and every time I pulled he grazed my nipple with his teeth through the silk. His fingers had reached my shorts, but he kept them over the surface of the fabric too, drawing closer and closer to the place I wanted him to be. *Needed him to be*. Waves of barely tolerable tingles shimmied across my skin from his touch and I didn't know if it was his magic or just how much I wanted him that was making them so powerful.

With excruciating slowness, I finally felt his finger brush over my sex, and a low moan left my lips. I heard his ragged breath as he must have felt how damp the silk between my legs was, and then he was kissing me on the mouth again, urgent and hungry. He tasted divine, and my mind blanked as his fingers danced like a feather over my most sensitive spot. The pressure was building with every movement, the desire inside me like a freight train, gathering too much momentum to hold on to. I kissed him back with a desperation I'd never felt before, as days and days of passion for this beautiful man, *this god*, flooded to where he expertly teased and touched me.

'Hades,' I moaned aloud, and a shattering wave of release crashed over me. His other arm wrapped tight around my shuddering body, and I buried my face in his neck, kissing any skin I could reach over and over as waves of pleasure hammered through me in shuddering aftershocks.

'Gods, you're stunning,' he murmured, his voice

strained. 'I want to feel you do that again, around me. I want you, Persephone.'

'I'm yours,' I breathed back, gripping his shoulders.

But he moved back again, looking down into my face as he brushed a knuckle across my cheek. His eyes were glittering with fierce passion, but his words were soft.

'I never thought I'd see you again,' he said. 'Let alone hear you say those words. I-I don't want you to leave.'

I stared up at him, trying to concentrate on his words instead of the pleasure still rocking through my tremoring body, my desire to touch him, to feel him inside me, for him to take me completely.

'But you said I couldn't stay.'

'I know. But, I can't do it. I can't let you go again.'

Something inside me sparked, and it wasn't connected to my desire. It was deeper than that. *I was happy.* I was happy that he didn't want me to go.

But that wasn't the plan. I needed to get back to New York, away from murderous gods and amoral assholes.

And leave your powers, underwater worlds, flying ships and a fucking god who wants to spend an eternity worshiping you?

'I- I don't know if I belong here,' I said hesitantly. Hades said nothing, but emotion flickered through his eyes. 'But I do know that I feel something for you. Something I have never felt before.'

'We are bound,' he said quietly. 'But you have not fully accepted it. If you do, you will feel it.'

'I already feel something.'

He shook his head.

'It is not *something*. It is everything.'

I didn't know what to say. Guilt washed over me.

'I'm sorry,' I said, meaning it. I wanted, more than anything, to make him happy. Not just because of how much I wanted him physically, but because it was unbelievably important to me that he was happy. That must be the bond he was talking about, I supposed.

He stood up slowly.

'I'll make you a deal,' he said. 'If the bond awakens, and you feel it, I'll do everything in my power to keep you here. But if it is truly gone, then I swear you'll go back to New York, with no memory of me or Olympus.'

I sat up straight, pushing my legs together. This conversation was no longer about sex. And I didn't know what I wanted anymore. As much of me that wanted to return home to my brother and my gardens, also wanted to stay here, to find my powers, be with Hades and grow trees for eternity.

But the thought of the Empusa's lair, the people in the hourglasses at the ball, Hades' own indifferent reaction to what the gods did for entertainment, all made me pause. *That wasn't me.* And even if it was, there was no way in the world I could live in this place, with no outside, no windows, and death and demons beneath our feet.

'I need to think about this,' I said. 'It's a lot to take in, and I only just got my powers back. I don't know my place here at all.'

'Your place is by my side,' he said tightly, after a long pause. Part of me agreed with him, instinctively. The part that wished he'd kept his gorgeous mouth shut and not started this conversation. But not a large enough part of me to be sure.

'How about we talk about this if I survive all the Trials?' I said as casually as I could manage.

'You need to win the Trials.'

'What?'

'If you do not, I must marry Minthe.'

A bolt of jealousy ripped through me at the thought of him wed to someone else, and I screwed my face up.

'It's not that easy,' I said. 'I don't know if you've noticed, but your brothers really don't seem keen to make my time in Olympus pleasant.'

'You need to win,' he repeated. Frustration welled in me.

'I haven't even decided if I want to stay!' Hurt flashed across his face, and suddenly his shirt shimmered back over his chest.

'You've been through a lot today. You need to get some rest,' he said, his voice awkward and formal.

'But-' I started, then flinched and looked down as I felt my fighting clothes reappear around my body. They were dry now. 'Hades, please,' I tried again.

'I lost you once,' he said quietly. 'I don't know if I can do it again.'

'Just give me a little time to think,' I said and stood, reaching up to touch his face. His silver eyes flashed with desperation as he bowed his head and kissed me softly.

'Just try to win,' he said. I stared into his face, my mind whirring.

If I really could win, and I did, then I would have the upper hand. I would at least have the option of choosing to stay with him, as unlikely as I thought that would be. The thought of him kissing someone else, lifting someone else into this chair, touching them as he had me, caused an undercurrent of fury to blaze through me. But that didn't mean anything, I told myself. He'd just made me feel freaking incredible. Of course I would feel possessive of him right now.

Even without Hades in the equation though, I was discovering that I had magic powers that felt amazing, and had glimpsed a limitless world beyond anything I could have imagined.

There was no way I was in the right frame of mind to be making decisions this huge right now.

But if I won the Trials, I would have time, and surely more freedom to make a real decision. A calm, well-informed decision that didn't hinge on fear or lust.

'OK. I'll try,' I said, and something fierce glittered in his eyes as he pulled me into him, kissing me again. I couldn't help the wave of happiness as I kissed him back.

If this bond he talked about did awaken, then I would have to deal with it then.

TWENTY-FIVE

PERSEPHONE

'So... we were in the middle of something,' I said, breaking off the kiss and giving him a pointed look that I hoped screamed *take my clothes off, now. Yours too.*

'Until the bond awakens, I won't lay another finger on you,' Hades said, cupping my cheek.

'Why not?' Disappointment crashed through me and the words came out as a squeak.

'Because I don't do anything by halves. When I finally get to be with you, I want it to be the most mind-blowing thing you've ever experienced.'

'I'm pretty sure you could achieve that right now,' I told him, thinking about the orgasm he'd given me without even taking my damned clothes off.

He gave me a long, penetrating look, then sighed.

'You really should get some rest. Hecate needs to teach you healing tomorrow, before the endurance tests. I've no doubt my dickhead brother has something horrendous planned.'

I briefly considered begging him to finish what we'd started, but my pride kicked in just in time.

'Fine,' I scowled. 'Can we walk though? I don't feel like any more flashing today.'

'Of course.'

We didn't speak on our walk through the seemingly endless blue-torch lit corridors, but it wasn't awkward. He gripped my fingers in his, and it felt nice. Better than nice. My body was still humming with all the power and pleasure I had experienced in the last few hours, the horror of the Empusa's lair starting to feel like a long time ago.

When we reached my rooms, Hades turned to me, and his face was steely and hard, and heat began to simmer inside me again. Strength emanated from him, and gods help me, it turned me on.

'Do not leave this room without me or Hecate,' he said.

'I know.'

'And again, I'm sorry in advance for whatever Zeus has planned for you. For what it's worth, he's not making me put you through any endurance tests, but I don't know which gods it will be.'

I felt a stab of relief that Hades wouldn't have to suffer through causing me pain or anger. Both for his sake and mine.

'I'll be fine,' I told him. 'I'll learn everything I can from Hecate about healing.' It was probably a good thing he had decided Hecate should teach me instead of him. My desire and confusion when I was around him would definitely distract me, and healing sounded like a pretty important thing to get right. 'Are these bonds always this impractical?'

'Yes,' he smiled, and kissed me, his lips like feathers and fire at the same time. 'But they say love conquers all,' he said as he broke away from me, then vanished with a flash of white light.

'*Love*,' I repeated quietly as I shut my bedroom door.

It hit me then. The reason he wouldn't be with me without the bond. He didn't want to 'do things by halves'. He wanted me to love him, as much as he already loved me.

Could I love him? There was no doubt at all that I wanted him, and that I cared deeply about his happiness. Was that what love was? I pictured his face as I leaned against my door. There was something so right about it. About him. And I knew there shouldn't be. He was practically the definition of wrong, he was the Lord of the Dead, a god who didn't mourn the loss of life, who shed corpses made of light as he tore humans apart, who instilled primal terror in his victims.

Yet he'd created an entire realm, and new species because of his craving for life. He'd never chosen his role, but accepted it because he had to. His realm housed outcasts without judgment, and didn't allow invasions of privacy like gods reading your mind.

I respected him, I realized. I admired him as much as I feared him.

The softness of his touch, the tenderness of his kisses, the intense emotion in his eyes, they all contrasted so bluntly with the monster he showed the world. Soft and fierce. Light and dark. Life and death. The Empusa had told me that I would not master the balance, and she was likely right. Had Hades nailed that balance, and hidden the soft side of himself away but kept it whole? Or was he just as in danger of losing his balance as I was?

'Is most of every god's life just parties?' I asked Skop as I adjusted the corset of yet another ball-gown. This one was bright red, the top half boned and tight like a classic corset, the bottom like weighted silk. White roses curled all the way from the hem up the right-hand side of my body. It was beautiful, but it was heavy and restrictive.

'It is when they're hosting these events, yeah. I guess that's why they have them so often.' I raised my eyebrows at him.

'Have any of the other gods been forced to marry like this?'

'Not yet. Are you ready for tonight? I doubt I'll be able to help you much.'

There was a bitterness to the kobaloi's voice again, and it was clear he didn't much care for being excluded from so much of my time with Hades. The suspicious part of me couldn't help wondering if he was reporting back to Dionysus. The trusting part of me wanted to believe he just cared about me.

'As long as you're not in danger again,' I told him, securing *Faesforos* to my ankle. My skirt reached the floor so the dagger would be unseen there.

Skop made a humpfing noise, but didn't say any more. I looked at my reflection, and took a deep breath. The red lipstick that matched the dress was far bolder than I'd ever normally wear but I needed to feel as fierce as possible tonight, and it somehow made me stand taller, and hold my head higher. *That's because Minthe was in red last time you saw her,* the petty part of my brain pointed out. *You want to look better than her.*

'*Are you ready?*' Skop cut through the thoughts.

'As I'll ever be,' I answered him.

Hecate had spent most of the day with me, trying to teach me how to access the part of my power that let me heal. When we were both pretty sure I knew what she was talking about, I'd very hesitantly made a tiny nick on my arm, and willed the skin to close. To my sheer delight, it had worked. And to my relief, she hadn't suggest we cause any bigger wound to test it on, but spent time talking about what it would feel like and how to draw more power to a specific area of my body if I needed to. I felt confident that I'd be able to help myself if I was injured, at least until my all-powerful god ex-husband got to me.

Knowing that Hades was looking out for me was a feeling I wasn't entirely used to, and liked more than I cared to admit. My brother had always been there when

I'd needed him, but we didn't live in each others pockets, far from it. Sam would help when I asked, but otherwise he let me stand on my own two feet. Which, to be fair, Hades was kind of being forced to do. He wasn't allowed to interfere in the Trials, but he had broken the rules multiple times already to help me.

If I was actually about to die, would he intervene? *Could* he intervene? Hecate said that Zeus was stronger than the rest of the gods; I assumed that included Hades.

Hecate flashed into my bedroom and my hands jumped on the dresser.

'Can't you knock!' I exclaimed. 'You frightened the shit out of me.'

'Oh yeah, sorry,' she grinned. 'You look ace.'

'Thanks. Any last minute tips?'

'Yeah. Put up with whatever they put you through, no matter what, and you'll win,' she said with a shrug.

'Right. Easy,' I said, rolling my eyes.

'And don't screw Hades at the party. People will notice.'

I shot her a look and her eyes sparkled with mischief.

'You're as bad as him,' I told her, nodding at Skop.

'*No, she's not,*' he said. '*Trust me.*'

Hecate seemed much more relaxed than before the last Trial, and I eyed her curiously.

'Why aren't you worried about this one?' I asked her.

'It's an endurance test, and you're strong. If they need

you to endure something, then it's not likely to actually kill you,' she said, flopping down on my bed.

'That's a good point.'

'*Although they might kill someone else,*' added Skop.

'Shut up,' Hecate said. 'Look, you'll go around all the gods at the party, and some of them will make you put up with something shitty for a few minutes. Done.'

'That doesn't sound like a good end to Round Two,' I said skeptically. 'I thought they liked more drama than that.'

'Some of them might be a bit nasty, I guess. But probably not as bad as drowning in Underworld sewage.'

'Yeah, not a lot could be worse than that,' I said, a shudder of anger taking me at the memory. I felt my magic simmer under my skin in response. I didn't know if that was comforting or alarming.

'*What if whoever left the doll and the mirror gatecrashes again, with something worse than a phoenix?*' asked Skop.

'Seriously?' Hecate glared at him. 'You're not helping, Skop. Hades' captain of the guard, a very stern Minotaur called Kerato, is all over it. There's no need to worry.'

The anxiety and nerves were building inside me, Hecate's blasé attitude not really settling me at all. I didn't believe for one second this would be easy. Zeus would want to end the round with a bang, I was sure of it.

TWENTY-SIX

PERSEPHONE

Hecate flashed us to a room that for the briefest of
moments, I thought was Hades' breakfast room.
But as I looked around, I could see stark differences. It
shared the towering vaulted ceiling, and the tall arched
windows covered by heavy drapes along one wall. But
the platform with the tree in the center, and the table for
two that should have been dwarfed by the room but
somehow wasn't, were very much missing.

Instead, a long row of twelve marble thrones dominated the middle of the room, running parallel to the
windows. There was a cold formality to the room that
made me even more uncomfortable than I already felt.
Where the masquerade ball had been almost ethereal,
with twinkling stars on the rocky walls, atmospheric
lighting and columns everywhere to hide behind, this
room looked serious and solemn. It was lit by cool blue
flames flickering in wall sconces, and waist high columns
with flat tops provided somewhere for guests to put their

drinks. And there were many guests. Faces that were now familiar peered at me from where they gathered in small clusters, all beautifully dressed in gowns and robes and togas that wouldn't have looked out of place on a catwalk back home. I clocked Selene, Eros, Hedone and Morpheus, and others I had last seen at the party on Aquarius as I scanned the room, smiling politely. The smile slipped slightly when I made eye contact with Minthe though, her eyes filled with malice. She looked stunning in a black strapless sheath dress, and my gut constricted as my confidence started to shrivel.

But then Hades' voice sounded in my mind.

'You look incredible. I love you in red.' I felt my back straighten, and my smile widen again.

'Where are you?'

'The gods are all here, we're just not allowed to reveal ourselves yet. My brother is a glutton for drama.'

'I thought you weren't supposed to talk in people's heads in Virgo without their permission?'

'Ah, I apologize. I assumed I did have your permission.'

'Well, you know what they say about assumptions,' I told him, accepting a drink from a satyr waiter who had appeared by my side.

'No. I have no idea what they say about assumptions.'

'Oh. That saying not made it from my world to here then?'

'It has not. Enlighten me.'

'They say assumptions are the mother of all fuck ups.'

There was a long pause, then Hades spoke again.

'The mother of all fuck ups is that pain-in-my-ass goddess, Eris.'

I snorted a laugh and Hecate gave me a slightly alarmed look as she raised her own glass to her lips.

'I guess the saying doesn't really apply here.'

'I guess not. I'll see you soon, Beautiful. Good luck.'

Hecate and I separated, and I did my obligatory tour of the hall, smiling and nodding at everyone I spoke to whilst sipping my fizzy wine. As Hecate had said there would be, there were many more guards than I had seen before, posted at each of the large doorways at the ends of the hall and lining the walls between the windows. The hall felt weirdly empty, despite how many people and creatures filled it, and nervous energy was crackling under my skin with increasing ferocity.

'It's so lovely to see you again,' beamed Selene as I reached her.

'And you,' I smiled, meaning it. She had been warm and kind to me at the masquerade ball, and I sensed sincerity from her.

'Don't tell anyone, but I rather think you've become Olympus's favorite for this you know,' she said conspiratorially.

'Seriously?' I blinked at her.

'Told ya,' said Skop in my head, and I glanced down at him, his tail wagging. *'I knew they'd all love an underdog.'*

'Watching you come into your power is a pleasure,' Selene beamed. I opened my mouth but nothing came out. Selene was one of the nicest people I'd met so far, and even she thought watching me nearly drown in shit and be eaten by a sea monster was 'a pleasure'. What the hell was wrong with the people here? 'I'm sure you'll do fantastic tonight,' she said enthusiastically, filling the gap I'd left in the conversation.

I felt a tap on my arm and spun around gratefully.

An enormous minotaur that I had seen a few times before in Hades' throne room bowed his head slightly at me, and I resisted the instinct to step backwards.

'*Dionysus drown me in wine, he's a big bastard,*' breathed Skop.

'You must be Kerato,' I said quickly, remembering what Hecate had told me about Hades' Captain of the Guard as I stared up at the minotaur. He was least nine feet tall, his hooves alone reaching half way up my shin. The beast blinked at me, his jet black pupils ringed with scarlet red. Hairy eyebrows cut above his eyes at an angry angle, and two curved black horns jutted from the sides of his furry skull.

'That is correct, my Lady,' he said gruffly. 'King Hades asked me to make myself known to you.'

'Thank you,' I said.

'Anyone wearing this sigil is part of Hades' guard.' He banged his clawed fist to the metal disc in the center of the gleaming armor that was strapped across his chest. A skull with a snake emerging from its left eye was carved on it. I couldn't help thinking that it looked like the sort of tattoo someone in a biker gang would have.

'OK,' I said.

'Good luck,' the minotaur grunted, then turned and marched back towards the doors.

'Quite intimidating, isn't he?' said a sultry voice, and I turned with a smile to see Hedone. She kissed me on both cheeks.

'He seems like he takes his job seriously,' I said.

'I've no doubt.'

'Where's Morpheus?'

'He couldn't make it tonight, but he wishes you luck.'

'Thank you. Hedone, what kind of creature is that?' I asked her as something with massive leathery wings and what looked like the legs of a lion stalked past us. His nose was a hooked, yellowing beak and his beady eyes swept over me as I stared at him.

'He looks like a Griffon hybrid,' she said. When I raised my eyebrows questioningly at her, she elaborated. 'There are wild and sentient versions of most creatures in Olympus, although some are more prone to staying wild. Like manticores. They are large winged cats with scorpion tails that live in forests, and it's very rare to find them sentient. But Griffons, who are lion and eagle, have enough human in them that most are sentient. It's rare to find them wild. His wings are large for a Griffon though, so perhaps there is some Harpy in there somewhere.'

'So a Griffon had sex with a Harpy?' I tried to keep the disbelief out of my voice as my brain went into overdrive picturing that union. The only harpies I'd seen here were mostly bird with human heads.

Hedone gave a soft chuckle.

'Where there's a will, there's a way,' she said.

'*There sure is,*' added Skop. '*I'm only three feet tall, and you should see what I've managed to bang.*' I rolled my eyes at him, but he just wagged his tail faster. '*It's all down to my enormous-*'

'Good evening, Olympus!' The commentator's greeting cut the kobaloi's sentence off, and it was the first time I had been grateful to hear the irritating blond man's voice. The room stilled, and I followed the collective gaze of the crowd to the middle of the room, where the commentator was standing at the left end of the row of thrones. 'Welcome to the last Trial of Round Two. And we have a bit of a twist for you! But first, please welcome your Gods!' The room dropped to their knees as one, myself included, as a white light filled the room. But I raised my bowed head enough to see Hades, his rippling smoky form on the far right of the row.

'Now, this evening Persephone will have to withstand four endurance tests, instigated by four gods,' the commentator boomed, as everyone rose to their feet. 'She can choose to go and talk to any god she likes in any order, but she does not know which gods will be testing her.' I cast my eyes over the gods' faces, searching for any giveaways in expression. I saw none. Not one even glanced at me. 'This evening though, there will be no judging,' said the commentator, and a ripple of chatter filled the room. *No judging? What?* 'Instead, for every test

Persephone fails, she will lose one of her existing four tokens.'

Dread trickled down my spine. Lose my tokens? I'd already eaten two, for gods' sake. Would that mean I would lose the power I'd gained back as well? Plus there were only three more Trials after this one, and I needed six tokens to win. I did the math fast.

If I lost only one seed I could still win, but I would have to get at least one token on the next three Trials. And as I'd already proven twice, getting tokens was not easy.

Anger boiled through my blood as all my hopes of only having to do two more Trials faded away. Not only could I not win any more tokens now, they were actually going to take away what I'd already earned? And possibly my powers too?

'This is total bullshit,' I hissed under my breath. The chances of me getting tokens on every single other Trial were surely slim to none. And even if I hadn't just decided that I wanted to win these cursed fucking Trials, there was no way I was losing my new powers.

I was going to have to deal with whatever they threw at me and keep all four seeds, no matter what.

TWENTY-SEVEN

PERSEPHONE

'Persephone, come forward! Choose your first god!'

Every head in the crowd snapped to me as one, and I couldn't help gulping. My skin was fizzing with nervous energy now, and I was uncomfortably aware of my sweating palms.

Those palms have freaking magic vines in them, you can do this! I repeated the words to myself as I strode through the parting crowd towards the commentator. When I reached him he beamed at me, teeth pearly white and perfect.

'Now, who would you like to try first?'

'Hades,' I said, without hesitation. *Was that smart,* I thought as a ripple of laughter moved through the crowd. He was the only god I knew didn't have a test for me. But his name had sprung to my lips and now it was too late to take it back.

'Very well. Go ahead.'

Carefully avoiding looking at any of the other gods, I

fixed my attention on Hades' smoky form and walked down the row of thrones towards him. I could feel the other Olympian's eyes on me, but I ignored them. The best way to avoid being intimidated or manipulated by them was to be in charge, I decided.

When I reached Hades' throne and stood before him, he reached forward, his translucent smoke arm holding out a small silver goblet.

'Drink from the cup of death and see if you shall be tested,' he said, and his voice was the nasty, slithery tone I had almost forgotten existed. This was the Hades the rest of the world saw. I took the cup from him, searching his face for any signs of silver eyes, but he gave me nothing. *He couldn't show any favoritism,* I told myself, biting back the stabbing hurt his indifference was causing. Slowly, I drank from the little silver goblet. The liquid in it was sweet, but not a flavor I could place.

'No test from Hades!' sang the commentator. 'Choose your next god!' I handed Hades the goblet back, praying for a glimpse of his true self. I only just kept the smile from my face as the briefest flash of gleaming silver eyes shone through the smoke as he took the cup from me, and a surge of confidence followed.

I could do this.

'Athena,' I said firmly. She was seated two thrones away, Ares sitting between her and Hades. The god of war was again wearing the red-plumed helmet that hid his face, and this close I could see how thickly corded his massive torso was with muscle. I would really, really not like to get on the wrong side of him. Or face a test from him.

Athena was wearing the same white toga I had seen her in before, her hair braided around her head. As I stood before her, a small owl seated on her shoulder blinked its large eyes at me.

'Drink from the cup of wisdom and see if you shall be tested,' the goddess said as she handed me a goblet identical to the one Hades had given me. I took a quick sip from the cup. This time it was bitter tasting, but nothing happened.

'Time to move on Persephone! Where to next?' The commentator's voice brimmed with excitement.

'Aphrodite,' I said, and looked five thrones down the line to where the goddess of love sat beside her husband, Hephaestus. If I was tested by Aphrodite, what the hell would that involve? What if she made me withstand something sexual? My nerves built as I approached her, panic that I might be put through something like that unwillingly rising in me. Hedone said that sort of thing wasn't allowed, I told myself, remembering the conversation I'd had with her before the ball about ego driving consensual sex in Olympus. The powerful liked to earn their good times, rather than take them.

Nonetheless, my hands shook as I took the cup from the goddess. She beamed at me, her vivid green eyes sparkling from under outrageously thick lashes, her hair jet black today, and cropped in a bob. She was wearing a skin-tight white dress and reminded me a little of Cleopatra. *Please don't be a test*, I prayed as I closed my eyes and took a sip from the goblet. The liquid tasted a million times better than the last two, but mercifully, nothing happened.

'Choose your next god! We're getting bored, Persephone!' I mustered up a dirty look to throw at the commentator, then handed the goblet back to Aphrodite.

'Dionysus,' I said, and moved back to where Dionysus was sitting, on the other side of Athena. I was unsurprised to see him once more in tight leather pants, a white shirt mostly open and only half tucked in. He had one ankle crossed over his knee, and dark sunglasses on.

'Drink from the cup of wine and see if you shall be tested,' he drawled, and leaned forward lazily with a goblet. I took it from him, for the first time knowing what to expect the liquid to taste like. Sure enough, it was a rich red wine, and freaking delicious. Before I'd realized what I was doing, I'd downed the whole damned glass. I licked my lips as I drained the last drops, and was just exclaiming how good it was, when I realized I wasn't in the hall any more.

That wasn't normal wine, I realized, spinning on the spot, panic flooding through me. I was in a forest. Except the trees around me stretched up so high that I couldn't see their tops, the light from the sky just streaking through gaps in the foliage. As I blinked around, I realized I could see little wooden structures high in the branches. I inhaled deeply, the smell of damp earth magnificent to me. Before I'd noticed I was doing it, green vines were snaking out of my palms, the lure of so much nature around me irresistible.

Then a low snarl snapped my attention to the nearest huge tree trunk. The gnarled wooden bark seemed to swirl and move in front of me, and I squinted at it. A wave of dizziness washed over me, as something black and lithe stalked from behind the tree trunk. Wings unfurled from its back, and I blinked furiously as the world tilted on its axis.

I felt drunk. Out of control drunk, not happy, silly drunk. I tried to focus on the thing now prowling towards me, and a flash of red above its back came sharply into focus all of a sudden. It was a glowing stinger, on the end of a scorpion tail. My conversation with Hedone earlier sprang into my mind, about winged cats with scorpion tails but I couldn't remember what they were called. A new disorientating wave of dizziness pounded over me, and I actually stumbled. Somewhere in the distance I heard a loud gong, then a voice rang out.

'Ten minutes, starting now!'

Ten minutes for what? I'd known before that I was here for something important but now... I struggled to piece together the last few minutes, but I could feel my memories slipping away as I stared at the huge black cat approaching me. He didn't look friendly. Maybe he lived in this forest? A woozy calm was settling over me, and I held my hand out, a green vine stretching towards the cat. He bared his teeth, and my vision wobbled again. A laugh bubbled from my lips. He was quite cute really, with his feathered wings and slinky steps.

Run!

The desperate thought pierced my cheerful haze, anxiety and fear smacking me in the chest so hard it was like I had been electrocuted. My feet started to move and I staggered backwards, my emotions flipping so far in the other direction that I was now too scared to take my eyes from the beast. There must have been something in the wine that was causing me to believe this thing was cute, because in reality it was damned terrifying. That bastard Dionysus had drugged me. My vision still swam, but I was sure the cat's teeth were growing, and its dark eyes were beginning to glow. There was no way I would be faster than it was. If I was its prey, I was in serious shit.

But its wings... They looked soft to touch, and were an ombre of reds. They were beautiful. Something that pretty wasn't dangerous, surely? My feet slowed.

It snarled again, dropping its shoulders low and pawing the ground and I felt another shock in my chest as the placid calm was dislodged.

Of course its damned dangerous, look at it! Now get the fuck out of here!

Before the lethal calm could take me again, I turned and ran for the tree behind me. I heard the thing roar, and praying I was far enough ahead that it couldn't reach me in one pounce, I launched my vines from both palms at a branch thirty feet above me. They flew fast, wrapping tight around the branch as they reached it, and I tugged, willing them to retract. I was lurched off my feet, my hair whipping around my face as I flew up towards the branch. I looked down, just able to see the cat past my billowing red skirt as he leaped for me and missed.

Within seconds I had reached the branch, and only then realized just how high up I was. The forest around me began to spin again, and this time I didn't know if it was vertigo or the drugged wine.

Your vines have got you, your vines have got you, I chanted in my head, but as soon as my addled brain pictured me falling, I felt the vines slacken.

'No!' I shrieked, as I started to slip, and they tightened instantly, wrenching my shoulders as my descent stopped abruptly. Heart hammering against my ribcage and my breath shortening, I forced them to pull me back up, then started trying to swing my legs up, attempting to hook my feet over the branch. Eventually, stomach and arm muscles burning, I managed to get my legs firmly enough around the wood to pull my body up and over the wide branch, my vines staying firmly wrapped around it too. Panting and nauseous, I eased myself into a sitting position, dimly noticing how torn my skirt was.

All I had to do was sit and not look at the forest floor below me until the ten minutes was up. It felt like I'd been here for an hour already, there couldn't be long left. A low roar snapped my attention to the main trunk of the tree and my vision wobbled even more as my blood turned to ice. The winged cat was prowling along the branch towards me, its massive claws gripping the bark like glue.

TWENTY-EIGHT

PERSEPHONE

Sense forced its way through the drug-induced fog swamping my brain as I scrambled backwards. It had wings, why the fuck did I think I'd be safe up a tree? The cat sprang forward, swiping at me with a huge paw, its glowing scorpion tail rearing back behind it. I ducked my body instinctively, fear of the cat overtaking my fear of falling, and it snarled as my right leg slipped and I cried out. Within a heartbeat my other leg gave way, not strong enough to keep me upright on the branch, and the world seemed to turn to slow-motion as the rest of my body followed my legs.

I couldn't breath at all as my fingers left the branch and weightlessness took me, the only thing in my head the certain knowledge that I was going to die. Then my shoulders wrenched again, harder, as the vines from my palms caught my weight and then I was swinging thirty feet above the ground, my whole body shaking violently and everything around me spinning.

I can't do this, I can't do this, I can't do this. The hysterical words pinballed around my head as the ground beneath me began to become obscured by the black dots overtaking my vision. I was going to pass out. And then my vines wouldn't stop me from falling at all.

Give up. I had to give up. *No, get to the ground!* The fierce voice sounded loud in my head, all the more shocking because it was my own thought, my own voice. *Extend the damned vines! You've already fallen from the branch, and you're still alive! You're stronger than this!*

Shaking my head, I willed the vines to grow, lowering me towards the ground. Looking down at the forest floor made the black dots come back, so I looked up instead, just in time to see the cat swipe at the exact spot my vines were coiled around the tree.

I willed the vines faster as his huge claws made contact, severing the vine from my left hand. I swung violently, but the right vine held strong, and now I was only ten feet from the ground and still moving fast. The cat swiped again, and weightlessness took me once more as I fell the last five feet to the moss covered earth. I landed awkwardly on my hip, and swore as I rolled and something hard cut into my thigh. Scrambling to my feet, I looked for the cat.

He was still up on the branch, but the dappled sunlight streaming through the thick canopy of leaves caught its stunning red wings as he extended them, then leapt from the branch. I couldn't outrun this thing, or hide from it, I thought, the pain in my thigh increasing. But as he landed gracefully opposite me, leaves swirling across the ground as his wings beat, the forest around me tilted and lurched hard, then vanished as a distant gong sounded.

I took a heaving breath of relief as the stark hall came into focus around me, the nauseating dizziness melting away fast. I'd done it. The ten minutes were up.

'Sorry, Persy,' I heard Dionysus' voice say, and blinked up at him on his throne in front of me. 'That's not how I wanted you to see my realm, Taurus. But I'm afraid I didn't have a choice. Nicely done though,' he added with a slow smile.

'Was the wine drugged?' I asked, trying to slow my breathing and willing my racing heart to slow down too.

'I happen to be the god of madness along with wine. Lots of Taurean wine causes hallucinations.'

'Wait, hallucinations?'

'Yeah. What did you see?' I felt my mouth fall open.

'You mean the huge cat with wings and a scorpion tail wasn't real?'

Dionysus chuckled softly.

'Had someone recently described a manticore to you, by any chance?'

'Y-yes,' I stammered, recalling the brief chat with Hedone I'd had before the Trial.

'Well, your sub-conscious remembered the conversation and your imagination did the rest.'

'So I was running away from nothing? I nearly killed myself in that tree for no reason?'

'I've seen people do a lot worse,' he said slowly.

A sharp pain in my thigh made me look away from him and down at myself. Through my torn skirt I could see a long gash on my leg, bright blood trickling down my bare skin. I summoned the power Hecate had taught me to access earlier, concentrating hard on the wound. Thrills of excitement pulsed through me as the skin glowed a faint grassy green, then began to knit itself back together. The pain faded almost instantly.

Confidence filled me as I watched my thigh heal. My most crippling fear was heights, and I had just fallen out of a freaking tree and survived. Not just survived; I hadn't given up. Last time, at the chasm, I'd quit. But this time I'd pushed through the fear, and won.

One test down, one seed safe, and now I knew I could definitely heal myself.

Bring it the fuck on.

'Hera,' I said, standing up abruptly before the commentator could say anything. I strode past Hermes, then Zeus, and stopped in front of the Queen of the Gods. She was wearing a teal gown that would be classed as a toga, but had a distinctly modern feel to it. Her black hair was piled high in a complicated collection of braids, all held in place by a glittering tiara with a peacock eye at its center. Her dark eyes glittered as she leaned forward and handed me a goblet.

'Drink from the cup of marriage and birth, and see if you shall be tested,' she said as I took the cup. I steeled myself, and took a sip. It tasted like blueberries. Nothing happened, and I handed her the goblet back and she nodded.

'Who next, Persephone?' called the commentator.

'Poseidon,' I answered. He was at the far end of the row and I marched towards him. Poseidon had already tested me once this round; I could handle anything he might throw at me.

'Drink from the cup of the ocean and see if you shall be tested,' he said, and handed me a goblet. He was in full god-of-the-sea garb again, sporting a long beard and holding a smaller version of his trident. Waves crashed in his blue irises as I drank from the cup. I tried not to pull a face as briny water filled my mouth, salt making my throat contract. But nothing else happened, and I handed him the cup back with relief. Artemis and Apollo were in the next two thrones, looking significantly younger and more cheerful than all of the other gods.

'Make your next choice,' said the commentator.

'Apollo,' I said, and the sun god beamed at me. He was shirtless, wearing just a toga style skirt, and his skin almost glowed gold, making him look as though he'd been carved from the precious metal. His body was so perfect that my brain struggled to register it as real. His face was the same, the planes so refined, the symmetry exact. Hades' muscled torso and beautiful angular face filled my mind suddenly, seeming so much more *right* than the underwear-model perfection of Apollo.

'Drink from the cup of the sun and see if you shall be tested,' Apollo said, leaning forward to give me a goblet. His voice was deeper, and older-sounding than I had expected it to be. I took a sip from the cup, and yelped and dropped it as searing hot liquid covered my tongue.

Heat, as though I'd just stepped into an oven, engulfed me. I groaned as I looked about myself and the hall shimmered. I'd just found my second test.

The world came back into focus and I found myself standing on a bridge, bright blue sky above me. Instinctively I gripped the thick rope handrails either side of me, and looked around, sweat gathering fast at the nape of my neck. The bridge I was on crossed some sort of wide crater, and as I looked down dread gripped my whole body. Between the gaps in the wooden slats of the bridge I could see lava. I was standing over a fucking volcano.

The deep red liquid bubbled and oozed below me, areas glowing bright orange and even white with heat. The boiling surface was alarmingly close, no more than fifty feet down. The more I stared at it, the more my body became slick with sweat, and the more oppressive the heat became. I turned as carefully as I could, looking both ways down the bridge. It just led to a narrow path that lined the inside of the crater. But could wooden slats survive this heat? If they gave out, I was toast. Literally.

A gong sounded, accompanied by the commentator's voice.

'Five minutes begins now!'

Five minutes? That didn't seem long. Rather than comforting, I found the shorter length of time distinctly unnerving. Something awful was going to happen if I only had to spend five minutes here.

Taking a deep breath of hot, sulfurous air, I lifted one foot. Except it didn't move. My sandals were glued to the planks, and panic fired through my blood as I pulled harder. An ominous creaking sounded from the bridge, and I froze in my attempt to free myself. Did I really have to just stand here, while the heat burned away the wood beneath me? I'd die, surely?

As my heart beat faster in my chest, I tried to take deep breaths, assessing my situation. Sweat was running down my spine now, as well as the backs of my knees. I could hear the lava gurgling below me. If the bridge was already here, then surely it was resistant to the heat, I thought, rationally. A cracking sound drew my attention to the end of the bridge, just in time for me to see the last plank burst into flame. My breath caught.

Another sound cracked behind me, and I spun at the waist to see the plank at the opposite end go up in flames too.

Shit. Shit, shit, shit.

This was an endurance test, I told myself, as the next plank along caught alight. The idea to frighten the participant into giving up. Not to actually kill them. I couldn't move from where I was, and there was nowhere to go. Which meant I had to hold my ground, no matter how close the flames got.

It turned out that was a lot, lot, easier said than done. By the time the planks four or five from mine were bursting into flames there was no part of me not drenched in sweat. I felt like I was suffocating, the heat a real, tangible, weighted thing bearing down on my entire body, crushing me. Every breath was hard, the temperature burning my lungs. And every plank that cracked and caught fire added to the heat and my mounting fear. My vines couldn't help me here. My healing couldn't help me if I dropped into the searing lava below. This was all about courage, and I was running out.

A plank three away from me on my right crackled with heat, then orange flames crept over it slowly at first, then burst to life, engulfing the dry wood. I turned slowly, knowing the opposite plank on my left would go next. Sure enough, fire flickered to life across the wood. Five minutes. I had to hold my nerve for five minutes, but I was estimating I only had about thirty seconds before the planks ran out and mine would go up in flames. And I had absolutely no idea how much time had already passed. The heat from the next plank on my left roared up, and I could smell the fine hairs on my arms burning. I closed my eyes, unable to watch as my mind begged me to quit, the fear bordering on winning over my willpower.

Just hold on, just hold on.

As if mocking my silent chant, heat suddenly

exploded under my fingertips and I opened my eyes with a shout as I pulled my hands to my body. The handrail was ablaze, and within a second the rope had disintegrated. My legs shook under me as the second plank on my right burned out. The heat was making my body weaken, all liquid inside me seeming to have turned to sweat. I felt the fire leap on my left as the last plank caught.

They won't kill you, hold your nerve. This is the only way to win.

It had to be the only way to win. They wouldn't make an unbeatable test, would they?

The skin on my face seemed to tighten as heat scorched up to my right, and I turned my face, closing my eyes again. This was it. If the next time I opened my eyes I wasn't back in the hall, I'd be dropping to a fiery death.

TWENTY-NINE

PERSEPHONE

A gong sounded, and relief smacked into me so strong I actually felt my legs give out as the world around me shimmered. My knees banged against the cold marble of the hall and a desperate urge to lay down on the cool stone swamped me. I took a huge gulp of cool air as a satyr trotted up to my kneeling form and handed me a large mug of water. I gulped it down gratefully, and wiped the sweat from my forehead on my arm, only to find my arm wasn't much drier. It briefly crossed my mind that I must look a hot mess, literally, with my hair plastered down with sweat and my dress torn to shreds, but the sheer fact that I wasn't burning alive dispelled my concerns quickly.

'My realm, Capricorn, is known for seasonal extremes, and I'm known for heat,' Apollo said, a rich seductive tone to his voice. I looked up at him from where I knelt, my body still burning hot and skin stinging and singed. I summoned up my healing power, but instead of concentrating on a wound, I tried to focus on my skin as a whole. A pleasurable tingle danced over me, followed by the feeling of cool water lapping gently at me, first over my face, then my arms and chest and back. It felt so good a long sigh escaped my lips. Apollo's eyes darkened. 'I could do that for you,' he said quietly. I pushed myself to my feet quickly, the predatory look in his eyes feeling nothing like when Hades looked at me that way.

'Thank you, but I'm fine. Just thirsty.' I felt a touch on my leg through my shredded skirt, and looked down to see the satyr holding up a refilled mug. 'You're an angel,' I told him as I took it and drained it.

Two tests down, two seeds safe. Two more to go.

'Where to next, Persephone?' boomed the commentator. I looked wearily down the line, then back. Between Poseidon and Apollo sat Apollo's twin, Artemis, her young and eager face infinitely appealing.

'Artemis,' I said, stepping towards her. A bow as large as she was lay tucked into the side of her throne, and her hair was as gold as her brother's skin. She was wearing leather fighting garb similar to what I had back in my wardrobe, and I felt a pang of jealousy. A ballgown and sandals had to be the least practical thing in the world to perform these sadistic damned tests in.

Artemis was short, and she had to lean quite far forward to offer me her goblet.

'Drink from the cup of the hunt and see if you shall be tested.' She sounded no older than a teenager. I took the cup from her, and took a sip, the word 'hunt' wafting through my mind and setting alarm bells ringing. The liquid tasted earthy, like beetroot, and as I lowered the cup my limbs shivered involuntarily. Was this a delayed reaction to the heat? I looked up at Artemis, her innocent eyes now glowing with a wicked gleam. Shit. This was another test.

The world around me flickered once more, and an endless, hilly moor materialized under my feet. The grass was brown-tinged green and reached my knees, and the air smelled faintly dusty. It felt like it hadn't rained in a while. My green vines were itching at my palms, the desire to nurture and grow the needy life surrounding me almost overwhelming. But that shivering feeling took me once more, and this time I could actually feel something skittering across my skin. My breath skipped in my chest as the gong sounded.

'Ten minutes,' the commentator's voice boomed, and I stared down at myself in horror as thousands of spiders scuttled from the grass and up my body.

A strangled noise crawled out of my throat as I started waving my arms wildly, vines bursting my from my palms and whipping through the air as my panic grew. Within seconds the things had reached my chest and were on my bare skin, and I shook myself harder as I stumbled through the grass, slapping at my arms and body, trying to get them off me.

'They're more scared of you than you are of them,' I panted desperately, repeating the words my mom had told me every time I found a spider in the trailer. But they'd reached my neck now and my skin felt like it was alive and I couldn't stand it. My own vine smacked hard into my shoulder as I beat at myself, and the force made me fall onto my ass. The moment's pause was long enough for me to take in my once red skirt, now almost black with hundreds of spiders, most tiny, but some enormous. A beast with red stripes and massive hairy legs skittered up my skirt towards my bodice and I shrieked as I bat my vines at it, again hitting myself in the process. My heart was hammering so fast in my chest I wasn't sure it could take much more. I'd have a heart attack and drop down dead under a mountain of fucking spiders. I struggled back to my feet and started chanting again as I spun on the spot, looking for any sort of refuge. There was nothing, not even a tree on the horizon, just a sea of dry moorland grass. I felt the tickle of legs on my bottom lip and whimpered as I clamped my mouth shut.

They won't kill you, it's an endurance test, I told myself, employing the same tactic that had worked when I'd been over the volcano. *Just ride it out.*

But my skin was crawling with spiders and it was impossible to ignore them, panic and disgust battering at my willpower like colossal tidal waves. I wanted the things off me, I wanted to be anywhere but here. They were crawling up the side of my face now and I knew they would be in my hair. I felt a hot tear slid down my cheek as I squeezed my eyes closed, the contrast to the skittering spiders stark. Revulsion gripped my gut as I felt something inside my ear, and I almost opened my mouth to give up. I had two seeds safe, I could afford to lose one.

Don't you dare! My fierce voice was back inside my head, and I tried to shift my focus to it, tried to ignore the feeling that the spiders were burrowing into my head now, through my ears. If I lost a seed then I had to win one in every other Trial, which seemed highly unlikely. And whether I liked it or not, something inside me had changed. I *wanted* to win. I wanted to have a choice at the end of all this, I wanted there to be a possibility that I could stay in Olympus. *Stay with Hades.*

Come on Persy, what can you do? I channeled determination through myself, trying to focus. Were my powers any use here? The vines were shit at keeping the spiders off me, but there was grass here. I willed my green vines to connect with the earth beneath me, still keeping my mouth and eyes clamped shut, my body frozen in place. The creatures were moving up my nose now, and I was having to breath hard through my nostrils to dislodge them. I felt sick.

Until my vines hit the ground. Happiness coursed through my entire body, the sense of space and life surrounding me forcing out the fear of the spiders just a little. I sent the eager magic I could feel building inside me towards the earth, willing it to find the grass, to fill it with what it needed to flourish. I didn't dare open my eyes to see what was happening, but now I could only feel the spiders that were still trying to burrow their way through my ears and nose, and the ones that had gotten under my corset. The rest I was able to block out. *How long had I been here?* Taking as deep breaths as was possible, I channeled my fear into the ground as life for the yellowing grass, the joy from doing so offsetting the revulsion just enough that I could hold myself together.

When I finally heard the gong I made the mistake of opening my mouth in a relieved gasp. I just saw the hall fading into existence around me as spiders flooded into my mouth. I coughed and choked, my vines vanishing as I clawed at my tongue, but the spiders kept coming. More tears streaked down my face as a sob was ripped from my throat, then I felt a cascade of something warm and soothing pour over my entire body, washing the spiders away with it. Weird tingles flowed through my nose and mouth, and when they stopped, I couldn't feel any more scurrying feet.

I looked up, still frantic, and saw that Artemis was standing up in front of me, a lop-sided smile on her face.

'I think that's got them all,' she said gently. 'And thanks, for sorting out my meadow. Sagittarius could do with some more flowers.'

'Flowers?' I stammered, trying to stop my body shaking and keep my dinner down. She nodded at me, and gestured behind her. A shimmering portal opened up, and through it I could see a meadow brimming with wildflowers, some taller than me and in every color I could think of. The grass was a lush deep green, and dotted with tiny daisies.

'Did- did I just do that?'

'You did. And you endured my test. Well done.' Artemis sat back down and I took another shuddering breath, still rubbing at my arms and chest subconsciously, and batting at my ears. I believed her that they were gone, but it still felt like I was covered in spiders. I would be burning this damned dress if I got through this. The satyr trotted up again and this time his tray had a small tumbler on it, filled with liquid. I took it carefully in my shaking hands and sipped. It was nectar. Immediately the shudders through my chest and limbs lessened. I felt my legs strengthening, and my pulse slowing. I looked away from the gods, towards the crowd, and saw Hecate at the front, giving me an over the top thumbs up, her thumb dancing with blue flame. Skop was sitting beside her, his tail wagging.

Three tests done, and three seeds safe. Just one more to endure, and I was getting in my damned shower for the rest of time.

'One more test to find, Persephone, which god will it be?' The commentator's voice was jarring, and I put the tumbler down on the satyr's tray. I looked along the row of gods, and they were all facing me. My gaze settled on Hermes' twinkling eyes and red beard, where he was sitting between Dionysus and Zeus.

'Hermes,' I said, and strode towards him with as much dignity as I could muster. The gods only knew what my hair looked like now, but it really didn't matter. What mattered was getting this Trial over and done with.

'Drink from the cup of tricksters and see if you shall be tested,' beamed Hermes, handing me a goblet. The liquid inside looked like mud, but when I hesitantly sipped from it, it tasted like cherries. I held my breath as I waited, but nothing happened. I let go of the sigh as I handed the messenger god his cup back, and felt a little buoyed by his encouraging expression.

I had Zeus, Ares and Hephaestus left. Frissons of nerves rippled through me as I thought about my choice. It seemed very, very unlikely that Zeus would let the round end without getting involved. Surely the King of the Gods was hiding my last test? If he was, I wanted to find out now, and get it done.

'Zeus,' I said, stepping to my left so that I was in front of the god. A slow smile crossed his face and his formal visage rippled and morphed into the gorgeous blond from the coffee shop.

'Drink from the cup of the skies and see if you shall be tested,' he drawled and handed me a goblet. I took the cup and started when electricity sparked through my fingertips. Oh, this was going to be a test alright. I looked into his eyes as I sipped the sweet liquid, and his lips parted.

'I'm afraid this might hurt a bit,' he whispered, and the hall vanished.

THIRTY

PERSEPHONE

I'd expected to find myself in an open space, or surrounded my lightning bolts like when Zeus had abducted me, but to my surprise I was in an underground cavern. In fact, it looked and felt like I would expect the Underworld to look and feel. I was standing on the banks of a river of liquid fire, which was running into a dark cave mouth in front of me. I turned slowly on the spot, thrown by how un-Zeus this felt so far. There was nothing else along the rocky river banks, and the high cavern ceiling sloped down towards the dark entrance before me. I peered into the river. It wasn't lava but actual fire, rolling and sloshing like water. It was mesmerizing, and I tore my eyes from it before I could get distracted. The only place to go was the cave, and I wanted this Trial over. So I strode towards the darkness.

The air was hot and humid as I stepped through the

arched cave mouth, and the darkness barely receded, the only light coming from the burning river.

I knew instantly that something was wrong. Seriously wrong.

It was as though my senses narrowed to slithers, only specks of sound making it to my ears, and flashes of images to my eyes. Despite the heat the hair on my skin rose, and I stopped moving. I tried to listen for the gong, but all I could hear were fragments of something high pitched, that faded away before I could work out what it was. Things were moving in the shadows, the flickering red light never staying still long enough for me to see what they were. Fear began to churn through me, my stomach tense and uneasy as my black vines slid instinctively from my palms.

Suddenly the flames in the river leapt up, and I cried out and staggered backwards as the scene in front of me was illuminated.

There was a shallow pool of water with an apple tree in the center of it, and chained at the waist to the narrow trunk was what must have once been a man. He was so emaciated his body was barely more substantial than a skeleton, his pale skin paper thin and covered in blistering sores. He stood rigid against the tree, his sunken eyes hollow and staring, his thin lips withered and pulled back from his teeth.

'Water,' he rasped suddenly, and I gasped in fright. *He was alive? How?* I watched in muted horror as the man leaned down towards the pool of water, his skeletal hands trying to form a cup. But as he reached the liquid it shrank away from him, as though it were alive. He let out a wracking hiss, then moved fast, throwing his arms up towards a low hanging branch from the tree, grabbing for an apple. The branch jerked out of the way, his fingers just scraping the fruit as it whooshed out of reach.

'They cursed me,' he croaked, his hollow eyes fixing on mine. I swallowed hard. 'I fed them my son, and they cursed me never to eat or drink again.'

'Fed them your son?' I breathed, very real fear now hammering through me, my vines hovering. Before he could answer, the flames in the river died down, and the pool and the tree and the awful man vanished.

This wasn't right. Where was the gong? And the commentator's voice with the time? What was I supposed to be enduring? Sure, I was scared shitless, but fear was Hades' power, not Zeus'. I needed to get out of here.

But what if this is the test? You can't afford to lose a seed.

With a snarl, I turned to the cave mouth a few feet behind me. Except it was gone. Panic mingled with the fear, fresh sweat rolling down my neck and making my palms clammy. I was trapped. The flames leapt again, before I could work out what to do, and where the pool had been before there was now a stone table. An enormous muscular man covered in dark hair lay prostrate on it, his abdomen ripped open. I heaved as a vulture swooped down out of nowhere, driving his hooked beak into the man's exposed guts, and he screamed. I turned my head so that I couldn't see, terror now taking over from fear as the giant's agonized shrieks continued. What the fuck was this place?

The flames died down again, and as soon as they did I dropped to my knees. There was no way I was walking through the darkness when I was surrounded by people being tortured. But crawling, I could feel what was before me before I reached it.

I'd barely moved a foot on my hands and knees, before the flames leapt again. My mouth fell open as a wheel made of fire burst to life high above me. It was spinning like a freaking firework, and strapped to its center, skin red raw and blistered, was a naked man. He was screaming the word 'Hera' as he turned and turned, the flames biting at his skin.

Something in my horrified mind jolted, a distant memory of my ancient history studies slotting into place. A man punished for trying to seduce Hera, strapped to a burning wheel to represent burning lust. And a man punished for serving his own son at a feast for the gods by being surrounded by food and water he could never reach. They were both sent to live out their eternal punishments in the depths of hell.

I was in Tartarus.

THIRTY-ONE

PERSEPHONE

I shouldn't be here. This wasn't part of the test, it couldn't be. Something somewhere had gone horribly, horribly wrong. I stayed where I was crouched, my eyes fixed on the grim burning wheel above me, my mind racing as fast as my out-of-control heart. I needed to get out of here. I was trapped in an endless pit of torture, and I needed to get the fuck out of here.

But there were no exits, no pathways, no freaking light. I was so far out of my depth I was drowning.

'Hades,' I whispered, his name coming to my lips unbidden. This was his realm, he was in charge. Surely he would find me here.

'Oh come now, don't be sad. We'll find plenty of people for you to play with down here, fledgling goddess,' a rich female voice echoed from the darkness.

'Who's there?' I called, unable to keep the wobble of fear from my voice.

'My name is Campe, and I guard Tartarus,' she

answered, and the man on the flaming wheel soared backwards as a creature I could never have even come close to imagining slithered into the space in front of me.

At least five times my size, she had the body and head of the most beautiful woman, full round breasts and a heart-shaped face housing deep brown eyes and voluptuous lips. But from the waist down she was made of snake. Her enormous lower half was that of a coiled serpent, and as the end of her tail flicked up I saw that it was itself made up of what looked like a hundred smaller snakes. As I dragged my eyes back to her body my gaze was drawn to what was around her neck. It was the most hideous necklace I'd ever seen, each charm lining the golden rope the head of a creature.

'You are admiring my jewelry? It is made of the heads of the fifty most dangerous creatures in Olympus,' she purred. I blinked as I took in the heads, a lion, a bear, a dragon, and many other things I'd never ever seen, and hoped I never would.

'Why am I here?' I choked out.

'That's not my business,' she said, staring down at me. 'But we rarely get such fresh blood down here these days. You will be a delight to the residents.'

'Residents?'

'Oh yes. You've already met Ixion up here,' she gestured to the man on the flaming wheel, 'and poor Tantalus, who fed his son to the gods. But the Titans rule

Tartarus. They are deep enough in the pit that they have not yet sensed you, but they will soon enough.'

The fear inside me was so strong that it had forced my tears and panic away entirely. I had reached the point bang in the middle of the crippling terror Hades caused that made me pass out, and the indecisive panic that burgeoning fear instilled. This was fight or flight, and there was nowhere to run.

I forced myself to my feet.

'I am a member of the Underworld palace,' I lied, with as much authority as my shaking body could muster. 'I demand you let me out. Now.'

Campe chuckled softly, the flames of the river dancing in time to the sound.

'A member of the palace? Those vines of yours certainly carry darkness, but you are not royalty.'

'I was,' I said, fiercely. 'And Hades will be pissed if you don't let me go.'

'Hades doesn't visit with us anymore,' she said, touching one hand to her cheek in a kind of mock sadness. 'Such a shame. I would be delighted if your presence brought him to us once more.'

So would I. In fact, I was banking on it.

'Why not?' I asked, deciding that keeping her talking was the best thing to do. It would buy time for Hades to find me. *Please, please let him be coming to find me.*

'He found himself a wife,' Campe said, bending at her huge waist and moving her beautiful face closer to me. The bloody head of a horned lizard bounced against her sternum. 'She became more appealing to him than torture.'

'I can't think why,' I whispered, staring at her morbid necklace.

'What is your name, baby goddess? It is uncommon to come into your powers so old, and you are clearly untrained.'

I scowled up at her. Would she recognize my name? Would it help me if she did?

'Persephone.'

A long hiss erupted from her, her genial expression morphing into a glare. Her tail lifted, the splayed end rippling as the snakes writhed.

'You are Persephone?'

'Yes, I told you, I was once royalty. Now let me go.'

'Ohhh, how I've waited for this day,' she seethed, her eyes flashing with anger. 'I don't think I will wait for the Titans to wake after all.'

I had about a second's notice, granted purely by intuition, to get out of the way as her tail curled around her body and came smashing down towards me. I tried to roll away from the river of fire, but I stumbled on the rocky ground and found myself shaken to my hands and knees as the ground rumbled with the impact of her tail smacking the rock. I launched myself back to my feet, my vines helping push me up, then began to run blindly as a low, maniacal cackle rose up behind me. 'I wondered where you were all these years, and now you just stumble into my domain. What a delightful twist of fate,' Campe purred around her laughter.

It was too dark, and I couldn't see anything as I got further from the river, Ixion's wheel high above me providing the only slivers of light left. A piercing scream from my right almost made me fall in shock, and a row of men seated on golden chairs flashed into view. Their faces were masks of agony, twisted and contorted with pain. I changed course, but felt something cold and hard smack into me from behind, then I cried out as I was lifted from my feet by an invisible force. I twirled in the air as I rose, my black vines now flailing around me, seeking the unseen enemy. I floated through the stifling air, coming to a stop before Campe, level now with her gleeful face. I was being held up by nothing at all, just like Ixion's wheel. My heart was thudding in my chest as I desperately tried to think of a way out, but she had been right when she'd said this was her domain. Her magic far outstripped mine.

'You took him from me, you little whore,' she snarled, and confusion bit through my fear.

'Took who?' I gasped, as I floated helpless before her.

'The king. He was turning. He was becoming what he was destined to be, and the glorious beast inside him was almost free. Then you took him.'

'Do you mean Hades?' I kicked my legs in the air, trying to right myself, to stop the slow spinning.

'Of course I do,' she hissed, leaning her huge face close to me. She smelled like rotting flesh, the iron tang of blood laced through the scent.

A roar bellowed from beneath us and everything around me, including Campe, shook as it reverberated through the pit. Her face morphed, fear actually flashing through her eyes as her cruel smile dropped. 'He is coming,' she hissed, then slithered backwards on her huge snake tail.

'Hades?' Hope soared inside me.

'No. Cronos.'

Cronos? Wasn't he the Titan who had eaten most of the Olympians? The worst of the lot?

'Shit, shit, shit,' I chanted as I willed my vines down towards the floor, searching desperately for anything to cling to, to pull myself down. But they couldn't get a purchase on the constantly changing surface, and it was too dark to see anything useful. Another roar bellowed around me and a new, more primal terror began to creep through my veins.

'Release her at once!' The command made me gasp in surprise, and I wheeled in the air, trying to see who had spoken. It wasn't Hades, but I recognized the voice.

'Kerato, how good of you to join us,' hissed Campe, who was still slowly backing away. Her tail was obscured by darkness now, her face and grisly necklace still flickering in the light of Ixion's wheel. 'Hades' lap dog is always welcome here.'

'I said release her, immediately,' The minotaur shouted. I couldn't see him in the darkness below me, but hope surged through me. I was no longer alone.

'If you insist.' My stomach lurched as I dropped

abruptly, my vines frantically trying to find something to slow my fall and disorientation completely swamping me. Then a blast of neon blue light blinded me and I froze in mid-air for a split second, before gently tipping forward and floating down.

'You will explain yourself,' hissed another voice, and this time relief hit me hard. *Hades*. As my feet touched the ground I whirled, then stumbled as I saw him.

He was in full-on god mode. He was almost as big as Campe was, shirtless and solid, blue light streaming from his body, and morphing into crawling bodies at his boots. I watched in awestruck fear as the bodies climbed to their feet and began to line up in rows behind him. An army of the dead.

'Hades, you're just in time,' Campe purred. 'Cronos is on his way.'

Fear and rage as real as I'd ever seen filled Hades' bright blue eyes, the usual silver nowhere to be seen. The temperature soared, and a jet of blinding blue light smashed into Campe. She screamed as she was thrown backwards, the necklace around her colossal neck splitting and animal heads flying everywhere.

'Get her out of here, now!' roared Hades, and I felt my arm being grabbed by a clawed hand. I turned, Kerato's horned face inches from mine.

'Sorry, my lady,' he grunted, but as white light began to glow around him, he bellowed and staggered backwards, releasing his grip on me.

'Kerato!' I shouted, as Hades' light illuminated the red blood dripping down his shoulder around the tip of a protruding blade. Then a cackling woman's face appeared behind the minotaur, her youthful, deranged eyes dancing with malice. 'Leave him alone!' I yelled, whipping my vines towards the new threat.

Another roar ripped through the space, and the fire in the river suddenly became an inferno, leaping a hundred feet into the air. Red and blue light crashed together, and I tore my eyes from Kerato to Hades. His face was strained, both hands held high as though he was holding back something I couldn't see.

'He's here. Kerato, get her out of Tartarus,' he said through gritted teeth. But the minotaur's eyes were glassy and he was clutching his chest in silence as the human looking woman stepped around him. She was wearing a black toga and her bright red hair was piled high on her head.

'Yeah, he won't be taking you anywhere,' she said with a shrug, and poked Kerato's shoulder with her pointed finger. The minotaur crumpled to the ground. 'The boss wants you for something special.'

'Who are you?' I stammered, eyes flicking between Kerato's body and her.

'Ankhiale, Titan goddess of heat,' she took a low bow as she spoke, and her black toga burst into flames. 'I'm responsible for the interior decorating down here,' she grinned at me. She looked completely fucking mad.

'Ankhiale, if you lay a finger on her, I will make your life a million times more miserable than it already is!' roared Hades. She gave another cackling laugh.

'You think that's possible, oh Lord of the Dead? Give

me a fucking break.' She was stalking closer to me, and I didn't know what to do. Should I use my vines, try to take her power? 'You won't be able to hold King Cronos back much longer, Hades. And you're breaking the rules, letting a pretty little thing like her down here. He won't obey you this time.'

Hades gave a wretched snarl, and I struck. With the tiniest flick of my wrists, I sent both vines at the woman, screaming as they made contact with her and heat seared through me like acid. But I held on, and the vines coiled around her shoulders, black tattoos blossoming under her flaming skin.

'What- how- get off me!' she shrieked, and gripped my vines in her hands. More heat, as hot or hotter than the volcano from earlier, burned along my vines and into my body, and the pain was almost too much to bear.

'*Get to me, now,*' Hades' desperate voice sounded in my mind. I did as he told me without question, letting the vines disintegrate as I whirled around. I let out a gasp of shock as I realized that the army of blue corpses were surrounding me, and as I pelted towards Hades, they followed, keeping their protective ring unbroken. I felt a blast of heat burn at my back and ran faster, throwing out a green vine and wrapping it around Hades' enormous leg and dragging myself towards him. The second my fingers landed on his body, the world flashed white.

PERSEPHONE

'What in the name of Olympus is going on!' roared Zeus, as the throne room materialized around us. I heaved deep breaths as shudders wracked my body, still clinging to Hades, vaguely aware that he must have shrunk because he was stroking a hand down my back.

'You're safe now,' he said quietly, pulling me tight to him. I felt like I was on fire, my stinging skin still burning, my lungs aching. Fear and confusion and pain were blistering through me.

'Answer me, Hades!' Zeus bellowed again, and I felt a crackle of electricity around us.

'Give her a damned minute will you!' Hades shouted. 'I don't know what happened, it was your cup she drank from.'

He tightened his grip around my shoulders, and I felt a tingle of magic wash over me, cooling my skin.

You're safe now. I repeated his words in my mind,

until I began to believe them, my heart finally beginning to slow its sprint around my ribcage.

'Tartarus is the worst fucking place in the world,' I mumbled into his chest, tying to suppress the sobs that the adrenaline and tension had brought bubbling to the surface.

'That's the idea. And you should never have been anywhere near it.'

With a deep breath, I pushed myself gently away from him, blinking up into his face. His smoky disguise engulfed him as I moved back, but I got a glimpse of his silver eyes, and the rage in them set my pulse racing again. This wasn't over.

'Are you suggesting someone other than one of us sent her to Tartarus?' said Poseidon's voice, and I looked towards the sea god. He, Zeus, Athena, Ares and Apollo were all standing up, every one of them looking alert and angry.

'Unless anyone cares to admit to playing a bad prank,' added Hermes. His usually playful smile was significantly absent. Nobody spoke.

'We will get to the bottom of this, brother,' hissed Zeus accusingly. Smoke billowed around Hades, tinged with blue light.

'Why the fuck would I do this?' roared Hades. 'Even if you rule out the fact that I don't want her dead, now Campe won't do a damned thing I tell her, and Cronos knows Persephone is here. You think I'd cause this shit in my own realm?' Icy cold air was streaming from him as his voice got louder, the slithering tone taking over. Zeus' expression changed from angry to wary as I watched. *Was Zeus frightened of Hades?*

There was a long pause, the tension practically tangible.

'We will deal with this in private,' snapped Zeus eventually, and sat down hard on his throne. The other gods followed suit, and Hecate appeared by my side.

'We gotta go,' she said with a glance at Hades. He nodded, and she flashed us out of the throne room.

We were back in my room, and the first thing Hecate did was give me a massive glass of nectar.

'Shit, Persy, Hades shouted something about Campe and Cronos. Please, please tell me you weren't in Tartarus.' I blinked up at her, and she shook her head and sat down on the bed beside me.

'*You have got to be joking,*' said Skop, jumping on my other side. '*You were in fucking Tartarus?*'

'A really big snake woman tried to kill me, then a goddess of fire killed Kerato while Hades held Cronos back, and then Hades got us out of there. That's the condensed version,' I said. A small sob escaped me as I remembered Kerato crumpling to the ground. 'He gave his life trying to help me,' I whispered, rubbing at my filthy cheek.

'Hades' guards are immortal, don't worry,' Hecate said quickly. Her face had gone pale again as she stared wide-eyed at me. 'Hades held back Cronos?'

'Yeah.'

'Persy, this is bad. Like really bad. Dying during a Trial is one thing, but becoming a Titan plaything in an eternal pit of torture?'

'Is that why Cronos wanted me alive? To be a plaything?'

Hecate didn't answer for a long while.

'Hades might know more once he's spoken to the others,' she said eventually. 'Have a shower, you'll feel better.'

I nodded and stood up, finishing what was in the glass and relishing the strength it gave me.

'Will you stay here?'

'Of course,' she nodded.

'Thank you. I really don't want to be on my own right now,' I admitted quietly.

'I'm not going anywhere, Persy.'

'*Me either,*' said Skop. Feeling eternally grateful, I walked to my washroom, pausing at the door.

'And you're sure Kerato will be OK?'

'Yes. It might take him a while to regenerate, but he's a demon. He'll be fine.'

'Ok. Good.' I turned and stepped through the door to my washroom, and froze in my tracks.

My apartment. I was in my bedroom, in my apartment in New York. My mind slowed almost to a stop as I blinked around the room. It looked like I had never left, the bed neatly made, a pair of blue jeans slung over the back of my easy chair, and my laptop open on the little desk, humming quietly.

I turned slowly on the spot, to see Hades standing behind me. I opened my mouth to ask him what was going on, but my words failed as I saw the look in his eyes.

THIRTY-THREE

HADES

As I watched her eyes widen in surprise to see me, I felt like someone had plunged a dagger into my heart. She opened her mouth, but didn't speak as she took in my face. My feelings must have been written all over it.

Devastation.

There was no other word that could describe what was churning through my ancient body.

'I'm sorry,' I said, my voice coming out brittle. Her features creased, a frown taking over her beautiful face. She had been through hell tonight, and she deserved to be treated like a victorious Queen. But we were here instead.

'Sorry for what?' she asked, her words painfully slow. She knew what I was going to say. I could see the fear in her bright green eyes.

'It's over.'

'What's over?'

'The Trials. Olympus, for you. It's over.' My voice was on the edge of cracking, emotion I'd spent over twenty years burying now building into a blazing pit of turmoil.

'No,' she said, and stepped towards me, shaking her head. 'No, you can't do this.'

She didn't know how close to the truth she was. If I didn't do it fast, I couldn't leave her here, in the mortal world.

But I had no choice.

'You wanted to come home. And now you are. It's over.'

Her eyes filled with tears as she punched out, hitting me on the arm.

'Stop fucking saying that! It's not over!'

Something white hot burned at the back of my own eyes. But gods did not cry.

'If I say you're done, then you're done.'

'Why? Why are you doing this? You said you wanted me to win, to be your Queen? You said Zeus had made sure I couldn't quit the Trials?' Tears were streaming down her cheeks, tracking filth from the pits of hell with them. The thought of her down there, in the darkest reaches of the most dangerous place in the world... The monster inside me roared. It had been awake since I lost her, since she had drunk from Zeus' cup. It had relished the fight with Cronos. And now I could barely contain it.

Cronos knew Persephone was in Olympus. Which meant she couldn't stay.

'I'll deal with Zeus,' I said quietly.

'So you could have sent me back all that time ago? When I actually wanted to leave? And you lied, told me you couldn't?'

'No. The other gods will back me on this. Zeus will have no choice but to abandon the Trials.'

'Will... will you marry Minthe?' Her words were barely audible, the pain in her expression unbearable.

I couldn't answer her.

'I can't believe you're doing this. I can't believe you actually made me want to win, want to be with you, and now you're fucking leaving me here!' She was shouting, her tears still streaming, her face furious.

I wanted to die. I wanted to throw myself into Tartarus's river of fire and burn to ash, rather than deal with losing her again. I couldn't do it. I couldn't see her like this, be the cause of her pain.

'*She will cause the end of Olympus.*' The words Poseidon had bellowed at me not ten minutes before echoed through my head. '*If she ever meets Cronos, we are all doomed.*'

I had no choice.

'Say something, you bastard!' she shouted, and another piece of my shattered heart splintered away, lost to the hungry beast inside me.

'You can't keep a light this bright in the dark,' I whispered, gathering every ounce of control I had left, and drinking in her every feature. 'I'm sorry.'

With a heartbreaking wrench that destroyed the last of my fragile grip, I left.

Someone would die tonight. Likely many. The beast inside me had broken free.

THANKS FOR READING!

Thank you so much for reading The Passion of Hades, I hope you enjoyed it! If so I would be very grateful for a review! They help so much; just click here and leave a couple worlds, and you'll make my day :)

You can order the next and final book,

The Promise of Hades, here.

You can also get exclusive first looks at artwork and story ideas, plus free short stories and audiobooks if you sign up to my newsletter at elizaraine.com and you can hang out with me and get teasers and release updates (and pictures of my pets) by joining my Facebook reader group here!

Printed in Great Britain
by Amazon